From the Ground to God

God

geveryl

This is a work of fiction. Names, characters, businesses, places, events and incidents are either the products of the author's imagination or used in a fictitious manner. Any resemblance to actual persons, living or dead, or actual events is purely coincidental.

No part of this book may be reproduced, stored in a retrieval system, or transmitted in any form or by any means, electronic, mechanical, photocopying, recording, or otherwise without the express written permission of the author.

DEDICATION

For my parents, Catherine and Harvey Robinson,
and my siblings, Lenny, Sheila, Jackie, and Alex.
Thank you for loving me from the ground to
God .

ACKNOWLEDGMENTS

Special thank you to Randall Kenan, Dr. Reginald Martin, and Dr. Barbara Ching for reading this story many years ago and for your encouragement. Monette Mclin, and Anna Kissel Fletcher, thank you for pushing me to release this book and for your positive energy. Dr. Uzzie Cannon, Rachel Jackson, Anthony "AJ" Joiner, John Robert Mayes II, Michael Northcross, and Wallace "Sib" Sibley, Jr., thank you for being the most supportive friends anyone could ask for, and Pablo, thanks for being the best dog in the world.

Jemimah

1.

I am a whore.

I wish I could say I *used* to be a whore, but I can't. I quit for a little while after Jake died, but money gets tight sometimes, and giving up tricking hasn't been as easy as I thought.

Jake was a pimp. Not your stereotypical polyester suit, gold chain wearing, yo, I keep my hos in check pimp though; he had class. And, he was F-I-N-E. Jake had mocha colored skin and hair as black and shiny as the Porsche he drove. He always ate at restaurants with names you couldn't pronounce, and he attracted attention from women *and* men. He even had his own designers because Versace and Armani weren't good enough.

There was another major

difference between Jake and the other pimps in the area; he went to *Queen of the Nail* salon every two weeks to get his acrylic nails done. They were always painted "Really Raspberry" (although at Christmas he'd switch to "Golden Swirl") and he spent a great deal of time at drag (as in queen) shows.

I'm kinda saved now. Well, I guess I'm all the way saved, but like I said, I slip up every now and then. My church is called Shepherd's Fold, and a lot of the members are ex-prostitutes and homeless people. We get to testify at church sometimes, and I love that. Most of the time when I testify, I talk about what I did/do for a living.

One time I told the congregation about a customer who would pay me $200 to give him golden showers all the time. It was kinda weird trying to explain why someone would pay to get peed on, but after church one of the deacons told me if he had known you could get paid that kind of money just to pee on folks, he would've quit his job at the post office years ago.

It's been sorta hard going from hooking to the Holy Ghost, but Minister Aiken (my pastor) says that as I get closer to God, I'll lose my desire for prostitution. I read in the Bible where God told this prophet Hosea to find a harlot and marry her.

He did.

Hosea told her she was going to stay with him and give up turning tricks. He loved her and took care of her for the rest of their lives. That's what I'm waiting for, my own Hosea, because God knows I'm tired of this routine. To be perfectly honest, I don't even like sex, but if staying on my back (or whatever position I happen to end up in) will keep my lights on, then so be it.

Last night we had mid-week service. Pearlie Gates, one of the new members, was there, and she couldn't wait to give her testimony. Her real name is Shalonda Mitchell, but she started calling herself Pearlie Gates after she got saved. She was wearing a purple spandex dress, silver platform shoes, and a "diamond" necklace, bracelet, and earrings. I could tell she had something really special to say because she usually didn't come to church all dressed-up. As soon as Deacon Sims asked if anyone had a testimony, Pearlie jumped up.

"Saints," she said, "you know we are truly blessed this evening. But before I tell you about the goodness of God, I want to give honor to my pastor, Min. Aiken, and all the Deacons, Elders, and

Mothers of the church."

Then she just stopped talking and stood there looking around at the congregation. Nobody said a word, and just when I thought she had changed her mind and decided not to speak, she said,

"Children of God, I stand here before you a changed woman. I'm changed because Jesus has come into my heart and made me new. People used to call me "Shay- Shay" when I was turning tricks, but I am now Pearlie Gates because I have been washed clean by his blood, and my coochie that was once paved with syphilis and other diseases is now paved with cleanliness and freshness, and I am disease free. I once was blind, but now I see, and I'm a sanctified ho now."

I heard, "Amen sister," and "Ain't God good," from members of the church, and I even had to say,

"Tell it Sister Pearlie," myself.

"Did y'all hear what I said?" she continued. "I said I am a sanctified ho and I'm trickin' for Jesus. Jesus is my pimp. Now some of y'all might think that Jesus can't be a pimp, but I'm here to tell you that he is."

I was really interested in that because I never thought of Jesus having prostitutes. I mean, I know he hung around them every now and then, but that was just so he could forgive their sins. I couldn't remember reading anything in the Bible about Jesus pimpin' any of them, but I haven't been saved very long so maybe I missed that part. Anyway, Pearlie was gonna explain it, and I couldn't wait to hear what she had to say.

"Before Jesus came into my heart," Pearlie said, "Bone Daddy was my pimp. He had control over everything. I gave him my money, my time, and my body. I lived for him, and whatever he said do, I did. But then, Jesus stepped in."

People in the church started standing up, clapping, and saying, "Preach Sister, Preach," by this time, so Pearlie kept right on testifying.

"Saints, when Jesus stepped in, he took control of my life. He has control over my money 'cause I make sure I give him his 10 percent out of every dollar I make. I give him my time 'cause I stay in the word, and I'm at church every chance I get to listen to Pastor Aiken spread the gospel. And, my body belongs to him 'cause I have been washed in the blood and consecrated by his love, and my body is now the temple of the Holy Ghost," she shouted. "Saints, I'm proud to be a sanctified ho, and

Jesus can pimp me for the rest of my life."

After she got finished, people were shouting and crying and saying, "Hallelujah." Pearlie even started jumping up and down, crying, and screaming, "I'm your ho Jesus. I'm your Holy ho now."

I started getting excited listening to her too, so I stood up, raised my hands in the air and said, "Make me a sanctified ho too, Lord. Please pimp me, Jesus." I knew exactly what Pearlie was talking about. Bone Daddy had never been my pimp, but when I first got started, I hooked up with this guy named Kilo.

I had seen Kilo around my neighborhood, and even though I didn't know what he did, I had heard that he was no good. As soon as he heard I had left home, he immediately offered me a place to stay. I wanted to say no, but I had been sleeping in the park and eating the leftover food from Kitty's Cafeteria for about a week, so I agreed.

Miss Andrea, a friend of my moms, worked at Kitty's, and she would give me the food they were about to throw out every night, if I went to the back door when they closed. I used to wonder why she didn't ask me to come stay with her, but one day, when she was giving me a carton of broccoli and cheese casserole, she said,

"Sugar, you know Miss Andrea loves you, and I would let you stay with me if I could, but you know Mr. Herman don't like kids, so I know you wouldn't feel right stayin' there."

Mr. Herman was her boyfriend, and they lived together. I remember how she would call my

Mom on the phone crying because Mr. Herman had been out with some "young slut." I never understood why she stayed with him, but maybe he was taking care of her the way Kilo took care of me.

I went with Kilo because I wanted to sleep in a bed instead of on a bench. To be honest, it was scary sleeping out in the park. There were always winos and homeless people moving around trying to keep warm. If I had been thinking, I would have waited until the summer before I left, but I was just trying to get away from my daddy, so I didn't care that it was February.

When I was at home, my daddy used to tell me I was so beautiful he had to fight to keep his hands off me. When I was 10, he lost that battle and started showing me how to "keep a man feeling right." After 2 years, I decided I had learned enough and took my newfound knowledge on the road.

I haven't been back since.

Kilo's place was nice, which kinda surprised me. I asked him if a lady had bought his furniture because his sofa was burgundy, and it had tan and green flowers on it.

"I don't need no woman to pick out nothin' for me," he said.

But I still wasn't so sure. He even had pots and pans in his kitchen because he said he liked to cook. The first night I was there, he cooked me baked chicken with scalloped potatoes and a salad on the side. He wanted me to eat because he said I was too skinny. He said I would be great for his business, and he was going to try to get me started in it the next day because he was sure I could make "good money." I really wasn't sure what his business was, but if it was going to make me money, then I figured it must be okay.

I asked him what kind of job a 12 year old could get making "good money," but he just laughed and said, "Don't worry about nothin'. I'mma tell you everything tomorrow. Just trust me, 'cause I'mma look out for you from now on."

I still didn't know what he was talking about, but I didn't say anything because this was the safest I had felt in a long time. I smiled, and then I gave him a big hug and a kiss on the cheek and said, "Thank you."

Kilo wasn't as bad as I thought. He even told me I could sleep in his room, and he would sleep on the couch. I was almost asleep when I heard him come in my room, though. He said it was cold and his heat wasn't working right, and he did n't want me to get sick. Kilo got in the bed with me, but he told me I didn't have to have sex with him if I didn't want to. I really didn't want to, but I was so grateful for everything he had done for me that I told him it was okay.

Sex with Kilo didn't feel the same as it did with my dad. Kilo didn't have a big hairy stomach that would almost crush me. He had muscles, and he wanted to kiss me while we were doing it. My Dad didn't kiss me at all. Ever. I hadn't really kissed a boy before, but I had seen it on TV. So, I just opened my mouth and stuck my tongue out as far as it would go. Kilo just laughed and said, "That's not how you kiss. Here, let me show you."

And he did.

It was nice. The whole night was nice because I learned how to kiss and how to really make love. What I didn't know was that the next day, I was also going to learn how to turn tricks.

2.

The next morning Kilo told me that he had some friends he wanted me to meet. He told me that they were having a party and they asked him to bring a couple of girls. I had never been to a real party, so I was excited until he told me what he wanted me to do. I couldn't believe the guy I thought cared about me would ask me to have sex with someone else.

"Kilo, are you joking?" I asked, hoping to God that he was. "How could you want someone else to have me? I thought you said you were going to take care of me," I cried.

"I'm tryin' to," he said casually, "and I can't believe you sittin' there cryin' like you didn't know what I was gonna ask you to do."

"How would I know you were

gonna ask me to do something like that!?!!" I yelled. "I'm not a whore, Kilo."

"You must be something," he said, "'cause I know last night wasn't the first time you had sex, and since you only 12, what else could you be?"

I could be a child who had sex with her father for 2 years while her mother watched TV in the living room, I thought, but I knew I couldn't say that. Or maybe I should have told him that, but it probably wouldn't have mattered. At any rate, I was out of luck. If I went back home, I'd just have to put up with my daddy and our nightly meetings. If I stayed with Kilo, I would have to have sex with strange men. I decided to stay with Kilo because having sex with my father, for free, was worse than having sex with strangers and getting paid. Besides, Kilo told me that sometimes the guys don't even want to do it; they just want to talk. I hoped I would get one of those kinds of guys that night.

I didn't.

I'll never forget how scared I was when we got to Jermaine's (Kilo's friend) house. He lived all the way on the other side of town, and it took us at least 45 minutes to get there. Kilo kept trying to comfort me and told me everything was gonna be okay, but I wasn't convinced.

"Relax and everything will be fine," Kilo said. "Just do it the way we did it last night, and everything should be alright."

I wanted to cry, but I didn't because Kilo had gotten one of his other girls to come over and fix my make-up, and I didn't want to mess it up. Besides, I didn't want him to think I was a baby. I just kept thinking about how good it felt being with him and prayed God would look out for me.

When we walked into the house, it was hard for me to see anything because there was so much smoke in the room. After a few minutes, I was able to walk across the room to an empty chair. Everyone there seemed to be at least 20 or 25, and I noticed a few of the guys looking at me. *Please don't come over here,* I thought, but they did.

"Hey, didn't I see you come wit' Kilo?" one of the guys asked me.

I just put my head down and started staring at the floor. I was hoping that he would think I was stupid or something and just go away.

"Hey," he said, as he leaned over and put his face about 1 inch from mine. "Didn't you hear what I said? I know you one of Kilo's girls, 'cause he told me he was bringin' some, but I ain't know you was gonna be so fine."

He had my daddy's breath. It was hot, and it smelled like beer, cigarettes, and rotten teeth. Every time I had sex with my daddy, the smell of his breath would make me want to throw up. One time I really did throw up, and I thought that would make him stop, but it didn't. He just kept on doing it, like he didn't even notice the corn and spinach I had vomited, running down his chest.

"Get up," this strange man said to me, and he pulled me up from the chair I was sitting in. "I wanna look at what I'm gettin' tonight." Then he started circling around me the way vultures do when they see something dead on the ground.

"Feel this," he said, as he placed my hand between his legs. "How big you think that is?" he asked.

I just stood there looking at him 'cause I really didn't know what to say. No one had ever asked me that question before, so I wasn't sure if he wanted an answer.

"How many inches I'mma give you, huh?" he asked again, and started rubbing my hand slowly up and down the bulge in his pants. "I don't know." I whispered.

"What did you say?" he asked and pulled me closer to him.

"I said, I don't know."

"Well, you about to find out," he said as he took my arm and started leading me to one of the back rooms. I was trying to find Kilo in the crowd, but I couldn't see him anywhere. I couldn't believe he would just leave me alone with this man, but I guess that's why I was at the party. After a few minutes I stopped hoping that Kilo would come to my rescue, and followed him into the room.

"What's your name?" I asked.

"Why you wanna know all that?"

"Because, if we're gonna do it, I think I should know who I'm doing it with," I answered.

"Baby, just call me Sweet Draws," he said, "'cause I'mma give you the sweetest, best, sex you ever had in your life."

He didn't.

First of all, that bulge in his pants must have been his underwear, because I couldn't even feel him when he was inside me. Second, he didn't want to kiss, talk, or anything. Then it only took him 5 minutes to get finished. I guess I should have been grateful for that though, 'cause that meant I didn't have to spend a lot of time with him. Or so I thought.

After he was finished, I asked him if I could leave, and he told me the party was just beginning.

"Baby, I got a whole bunch of guys waiting to be with you," he said.

"What do you mean?" I asked, trying to keep the fear out of my voice.

"I'll show you," he said, while walking to the closet. When he opened the door, naked guys came out of the closet and over to the bed. They were trying to figure out who was gonna get me next, and when they couldn't choose, they decided to all have sex with me at the same time.

I thought they were gonna tear my body apart. One guy grabbed me by my hair and pulled me off the bed and onto the floor, while the others kept saying, "Give it to her rough." Then Sweet Draws asked me if I knew what a golden shower was. At that time, I didn't, and I tried to shake my head, "No," but before I could, he started peeing on my chest and in my face. I wanted to scream, but I was afraid to open my mouth.

Two of the other guys must have gotten really aroused watching Sweet Draws 'cause they came over to me and started biting my breasts and licking the pee off of them. I started to scream when they bit my breasts, and Sweet Draws slapped me across the face and told me to shut up. By this time, the first guy, who had pulled me on the floor, started spreading my legs. I thought he was gonna have sex with me, but instead, he got a lighter from off the dresser and started burning my pubic hairs.

I was screaming, "Kilo, Kilo!!" but I don't think he heard me. Besides, every time I screamed his name, Sweet Draws would hit me in the face. I could feel myself losing consciousness, but I didn't want to blackout. I didn't want to die, not like that. *Where is Kilo? Why doesn't he come and get me?* I thought. I knew he must not have known what these people were like, otherwise he wouldn't have left me alone with them. I meant something to him. He told me so when we were making love. He'd come and get me. I just needed to yell a little louder.

"Kilo, please help me!" I yelled as loudly as I could.

"You think Kilo gonna help you?" one of them said. "Who you think told us about you? Who you think set this whole thing up? Now shut up and do what you came here to do."

At that moment, I missed my mother more than ever before. She died 3 weeks after I left home.

Everyone tried to say she died of a broken heart because she didn't know where I was, like it was my fault. But she used my Daddy's .38 to blow her brains out. She killed herself wearing her wedding gown and holding my baby picture in her hand. The note she left behind had my Daddy's name on it and just one word, "Why?" But that didn't matter. None of that mattered because the only thing I knew was that my mother was gone and those men were hurting me more than I thought possible.

"Please, please," I begged, as I felt one of them ram himself deep inside me. "

"I aim to," he said.

And that was the last thing I remembered.

It took me 2 weeks to recover from that night. When I woke up, I was back at Kilo's apartment, but I didn't know how I had gotten there. He had cooked some homemade chicken noodle soup and was trying to feed me. I was so angry with him that I refused to open my mouth out of spite, even though I was hungry. He looked at me for a few minutes and then he said, "Look, I'm really sorry about what happened the other night. I had no idea things were gonna get so rough."

"They said you knew what was going to happen."

"Do you think I knew they were gonna beat on you like that?" he asked. He looked so sincere that I almost believed him, but I still wasn't sure.

"I was calling for you Kilo, why didn't you come and get me? Why did you leave me with them?" I was trying hard not to cry, but the memory of that night was too overwhelming, and before I knew it, I was crying uncontrollably. I didn't want him to touch me, but I didn't pull away when he pulled me close to him though.

"I swear to God that I will never let anything like that happen to you again," he whispered in my ear as he gently stroked my hair.

3.

For 3 years I worked for Kilo turning tricks. He kept his promise because I was never beaten (at least not violently) again. However, I was peed on, peed on people, made to recite the 23 Psalm during sex (he was a minister) and asked by my johns to wear everything from a nun's habit to a prison uniform. I really didn't enjoy the sex, but fortunately a lot of the time, most of the men just wanted to talk or watch me undress in front of them. I can't say I enjoyed what I did because I didn't, but Kilo treated me okay, and I couldn't think of another job I could get making $500.00 a day.

Besides, if I hadn't been turning tricks, I never would have met Jake, the person who would change my life. I was coming from a john's house, when I made a wrong turn down a side street and got lost. That's when I saw him. He was coming out of Queen of the Nail salon. I was only 15 at the time, but I had been turning tricks for years, so I looked a lot older. *My God,* I thought, *I have got to get in his pants.* I usually didn't have to ask men to have sex with me because I got plenty of offers, even when I wasn't hooking.

Anyway, I wanted Jake more than anyone in my life, so I walked up to him and asked him for sex. Actually, I told him I wanted to ride him like Bronco Billy because I was sure that *that* would turn him on. He stared at me for what seemed like hours and then turned around and went to his car. I was speechless. Never had a man totally ignored me. I don't care if I am a whore; I've still got my pride, so I followed him.

Maybe he didn't hear me, I thought. But, when he got in his car, he rolled down the window, handed me some money and said, "Go get your nails done," and then he drove off.

Go get your nails done? Go get your nails done?!? I just offered this guy the best sex of his life…for free, and he tells me to get my nails done.

Needless to say, I was pissed. I stared at the money he had given me and realized that it had to be close to $200.00. For a minute I forgot I had just been insulted and thought about what I would do with it. I decided to take his advice. Obviously he had to be checking me out to even notice that my nails were a wreck. That had to be what turned him off. I thought he probably was some kind of finger freak and wanted my hands to look pretty before we did it. Well, I was definitely game, so I went to the salon.

When I walked into the salon, I saw 3 of the tallest (and the most beautiful) women I had ever seen in my life. They didn't notice I was there at first because the tallest one, who had blonde hair, was arguing with the other tall (but shorter) one who had black hair, and who was wearing 5 inch black platform shoes.

"Look honey," Blondie said, "I don't care what you say, that Shulamite woman was stank."

"Coco," Platforms said to Blondie, "how in the world can you call one of the greatest love stories ever told, dirty?"

"I didn't call the *love story* dirty. I just said Shula baby was a ho."

"Well Coco," now the third tall lady who also had black hair, but hers was cut really, really short and she wasn't wearing any shoes, got into the conversation.

"The Shulamite lady was just trying to tell Solomon how much she loved him. I don't see anything wrong with that. The only thing wrong with this whole conversation is the fact that Jake started this Bible debate, or whatever it is, then left. I don't know why he always has to come in here quoting scriptures and acting like he's Billy Graham or somebody."

"Don't try to change the subject," Coco said, "Jake might have started this conversation, but I'm gonna finish it. He said the Shulamite woman was not in love with Solomon, she was obsessed, and I think he's right. Now, as I was saying, Shula ain't have no business running around talking about her breasts were pomegranates. That is just nasty. Nobody wants to hear about her fruity chest."

"She didn't say her breasts were pomegranates," No Shoes said, "Solomon said her temples were *like* pomegranates and her *breasts* were like 2 fawns."

"Fawns!!" Coco screamed, "Do you know how big a fawn is? Don't nobody in the world have titties that big!"

"Coco," Platforms said, "can we please sit down and try to talk about this rationally. Better yet, why don't we just squash this entire conversation? It's silly. Besides, you know Jake is weird, even for us. Just drop it Coco." Platforms was obviously trying to calm this Coco woman down, but the softer her voice got, the more irritated Coco looked.

"I got your rational," Coco said. "Let me find my Bible, and we will settle this right now." After she said that, she started fumbling around in her make-up bag until she found her Bible. Then she walked over to Platforms, handed her the Bible, and said, "Here, read this." Now by this time, Platforms was totally pissed, but she took the Bible and started reading anyway.

"'By night on my bed

I sought the one I love:

I sought him, but I did not find him.

'I will rise now.' I said 'And go about the city;

In the streets and in the squares I

will seek the one I love.

The watchmen who go about the city found me:

I said, 'Have you seen the one I love?'"

After Platforms finished reading, she just gave Coco this crazy look and said, "And?"

"And?!" Coco said. "Hello?! Can you say stalker?"

"Oh, my God," Platforms said, then she started walking to the back of the salon towards a door that had DIVAS written on it.

"You can 'Oh my God,' all you want too," Coco yelled after her, "but I'm right."

Just then Coco turned around and looked right at me. I was so scared I almost ran out of the salon. But, before I could turn to run she said, "Hey, do you read the Bible?"

"S-S-Sometimes," I stuttered, trying hard to forget I had to pee. "My mom used to read it to me when I was little."

"Okay. Fine. Maybe you'll understand what I'm trying to say, since it is obvious that I work with heathens. Come over here and sit down."

I did.

"Now, "she continued, "isn't it clear to you that this Shulamite person was crazy? I mean think about it. Girlfriend got out of her bed in the middle of the night, and went running around the city asking strangers if they had seen her man. Obviously Solomon didn't want to be found. I bet while she was running around asking folks where her man was, he was with some woman who didn't have fawns on her chest. And when she did find him, she held him hostage and had sex with him on her mama's bed! Oh, she was definitely living foul."

I was trying to pay attention to what she was saying, but I couldn't because she was massaging my hands. I had never been to a nail salon before, so I had never had my hand massaged (well, at least not like that). I was really starting to get into it, and then suddenly she stopped rubbing my fingers and asked me why I was there.

"That guy who just left gave me some money and told me to come here," I said.

"You mean Jake?" she asked.

"I don't know what his name is," I said. "I just know he is fine, and I think he likes me."

Now you would have thought I told her a joke because when I said that, she just threw her head back and started cracking up laughing. I asked her what was so funny, but she didn't hear me 'cause she was laughing too hard. After what seemed like a few minutes, she controlled herself and said, "Honey, believe me, you ain't got nothing that Jake would want. As a matter of fact, you and Jake are looking for the same thing, so don't think he likes you because he gave you money. Jake is a pimp, sweetheart. He gives all his 'prospects' money. This must be your first time in this part of town."

I hadn't been in that area

before, but I didn't want to let her know that the only reason I was there was because I had gotten lost leaving a johns house. Besides, I was too busy thinking about what she had said. If Jake and I wanted the same thing, then he must be gay, which would explain why he wasn't immediately attracted to me. I had never heard of a gay pimp, but I figured anything was possible.

"How do you know Jake is gay?" I asked.

Coco just looked at me like I was from Jupiter and then she said, "What's your name?"

"Jem."

"Gem, like a jewel?" she asked. "Well, that's different."

"Not G-E-M," I said. "J-E-M. It's short for Jemimah."

"Jemima!! Like the fat Black

lady on the pancake box?" she asked in shock. "Your mama was trippin' when she named you." Then she started to laugh.

I always hated telling people my real name because they usually did the same thing Coco had just done. I don't even know why I told her, but it was too late now. My mom would never be stupid enough to name me after pancakes. Any other time, I'd just let the person laugh and make jokes about my name, but since I didn't have any more johns until later, I decided to tell her why my mom named me that.

"Not Jemima the pancake lady," I explained, "Jemimah in the Bible. She was one of Job's daughters."

"Uh honey, I hate to tell you this," Coco said, "but all of Job's children died."

"Yeah, but he got new ones when he got better," I said. "See, he had 3 daughters, and the first one was named Jemimah. My mom used to tell me that Job's daughters were the most beautiful women in the world, and Jemimah was the prettiest of them all. That's why she named me Jemimah, 'cause I was her first, and I was beautiful."

I didn't know what she was going to say, so I just sat there. Coco just stared at me, then she reached her hand across the table towards my face. At first, I thought she was gonna hit me, but she just rubbed my cheek and said, "She was right. You are beautiful, but girlfriend…you are wrong for those fingernails." Then she went to work on my hands.

She talked almost nonstop for the next hour, and it wasn't until she lifted up her dress because she had to "reposition her equipment," that I realized Coco was a man. *Platforms and No Shoes must be men too*, I thought. Needless to say, I felt really stupid. I didn't say anything, though. I just sat there thinking things couldn't get any weirder than they already were, but I was wrong.

Because by the time she got finished giving me my first set of acrylic nails (they were painted Pearl Glimmer), I knew 2 things.

One: my nails looked great.

Two: Jake was a woman.

4.

I thought I was a lesbian.

I had to have been because I was attracted to Jake, and he was a woman. I wasn't really sure about the rules of being a lesbian. I didn't know if you were considered to be one if you didn't know the person you were attracted to was a female. It's not like there is lesbian rulebook or anything, so for a few days I wondered if after 15 years of liking boys I was really gay, or just seriously confused.

In the 3 years since I discovered Jake was a woman, I've wondered if maybe, subconsciously I knew all along. I mean if there is one thing a prostitute knows (or should know) is a man when she sees one. However, Coco and the rest of the girls had me fooled, so maybe I wasn't as good of a hooker as I thought.

It's funny how things just pop into your mind. I hadn't thought about how I felt when I learned Jake wasn't a man for a long time, and then I started thinking about it while I was in church of all places. It was a Thursday night at mid-week service. There weren't many people there that night, and I wondered if it was because it was raining outside. Most people would stay home when it rains, but I've always loved the rain. I think it's romantic, and I love the way the grass and trees smell after a storm. But that's just me.

Anyway, Deacon Andrews was about to testify and although he's a little off (he's spent a few years in a mental institution) I love to hear him talk. Although most people say he talks in riddles, I think the things he says make a lot of sense.

"I was in a hole." That's how he began his testimony. "I was in a big ole dirty black hole, and the more I tried to escape," he said, "the deeper the hole got. I was trying to get out, but each time I thought I had escaped the blackness, it would get blacker and blacker. I kept saying to myself, 'I gotta find the white side. I gotta find the light,' but for years I couldn't find it. I thought I was never gonna escape until I finally realized that a black hole was just the darker side of the white hole. Do you know what I'm saying, church?"

Well, of course nobody really said anything. I mean, I heard a few of the deacons say, "Amen Brother Andrews," but that was about it. I think that black hole thing had everybody confused, but since he wasn't finished talking, I was sure he would try to explain what he meant.

"The black hole was the dark side of the white hole, which meant they were the same thing. I was just

on the wrong side of the right hole,"
he continued. "That's why I kept
drinking and gambling and doing all
sorts of terrible things. People
thought I was crazy, but I was just
trying to find the white side of my
black hole. Isn't that what we all do?
Aren't we all trying to find our way
to the right side of our wrongness?
But we can't do it. I couldn't do it.
It wasn't until I understood that
Jesus made the hole, and he was the
only one who could tell me how to
get out of it, that I began to see the
light."

Okay, now I wasn't expecting
him to say that, but like I said before,
it made sense. I could see the
members of the church start to perk
up and pay attention to him. And,
Sister Turner, who usually sleeps
through most of the services, even
stayed awake. I couldn't wait to hear
what he was going to say next.

"Church," he said, "all you have to do is reach up, raise your hands in the air and say, 'Here I am Lord. Save me from this hole,' and Jesus will be right there. He pulled me out, and he can do the same thing for anybody else who needs to be saved."

Now this time, everybody understood what Deacon Andrews was saying because everybody in the church was on their feet with their hands lifted in the air saying, "Thank you Jesus for saving me," and "Hallelujah." Deacon Andrews went quietly back to his seat and just sat there watching everybody else. I wanted to go over to him right then and tell him that I was still trying to find the right side of my wrongness, but I didn't. Instead, I just looked at him and smiled. After a few minutes, though, I gathered up the nerve to tell him that I needed to get out of my hole.

"Well, Jem, just get to gettin' the gettin' that's got to be got," he said, as he turned and walked away from me.

I would, I thought, *if I knew what to get.*

It wasn't until later that night that I remembered what I had been thinking about before Deacon Andrews began testifying. It was almost funny to think that I actually believed for a minute that I was gay. But, considering the circumstances, I think anyone may have been a little confused.

After Coco told me about Jake, I became obsessed with him. I wanted to know everything there was to know about this strange person. Why would any woman want to be a man, especially a woman as beautiful as Jake? Where were his breasts? I mean, I've seen flat chested women before, but none as flat as his. Did he tie them down, or had he had surgery to have them made smaller? Was Coco playing a trick on me? I knew the only way I was going to find out anything else about him was to keep going to the salon with the hope of running into him there.

For a few days, I kept trying to call Queen of the Nail to make an appointment, but every time I called, no one answered the phone. I knew Coco wouldn't see me if I didn't have an appointment, or at least called her first, but I had to see if Jake was there. So, I went to the salon unannounced.

When I got there, No Shoes came to the door and just stood there looking at me as if I were from Pluto.

"Is Coco here?" I asked, trying not to sound too afraid.

"Do you see her?" she said, and slammed the door in my face.

Now, I started to turn around and run away as fast as I could, but I had to find Jake. I had to know where he was and when he would be there, so I rang the bell again. When No Shoes came to the door this time, she looked really pissed, so I decided I needed to talk real fast.

"Look," I said, "I've been trying to call to make an appointment for the last couple of days, but every time I call, no one is here. I just want to get my nails done again, and since Coco did them for me the last time, I wanted her to do them for me again. If she's going to be here sometime today, I would really like to see her, you know, talk to her so she can do my nails again. That's all I want, I swear."

"She's not here," she said, "and even if she was, she wouldn't want to see you because she doesn't see anyone without an appointment."

"But I was trying to call," I explained. "It's not my fault no one was here. Look at my hands," I said, as I held them out for her to see. "My nails look terrible. All I need is for Coco to do them for me."

No Shoes took one look at my fingernails, sucked her teeth and said, "Look, Jem."

She knows my name, I thought.

"You are either deaf, or the stupidest person I have ever met. How many times do I have to tell you that Coco isn't here? She won't be back for a few days, so you're just going to have to keep those crusty looking fingernails a little while longer. Now, if you'll excuse me, I have things to do." And then she slammed the door in my face again and left me standing outside feeling like a complete idiot.

It was obvious that I wasn't

going to see Coco or Jake, so I went back home. When I got there, Kilo wasn't around which was a little strange. Kilo hardly ever left the house. I don't know if he was afraid someone would try to get him or not, or if he just didn't like being around people, but the only time he would leave would be to take one of his girls to a party to meet a john, or when he went to buy groceries. He had cooked dinner, and I was glad. I wanted to wait for him to come home before I ate, though because we always ate dinner together.

I've heard other people talk about how cruel their pimps were to them, but Kilo never hurt me or made me feel like I had to be afraid of him. Sure, I went out and turned tricks for him, but I got to keep some of the money, and every now and then, he let me keep most of the money I made. In a weird kind of way, Kilo and I had formed our own kind of family.

By 9 o'clock, I really started getting worried. I couldn't call the police because of what Kilo did for a living. Cops wouldn't want to find a missing pimp, so I decided to sit there and wait for him to come home, or at least call. I was supposed to meet a john at 10:00, but I couldn't leave until I knew Kilo was all right. Besides, I didn't think he would be upset about me missing a trick because I was worried about him.

I sat down on the couch and turned on the television. I didn't usually watch TV, but tonight I needed something to keep me company. Actually, I was a little afraid to be at home by myself, and the TV would keep my mind off the fact that I was alone. I must have dozed off though because the next time I looked at the clock it was 2 a.m. I really got worried then because Kilo would have never stayed away all night without calling me. Even when he was out with a girl or making a run or whatever he had to do, he always called. At first, I thought about calling some of his "friends" to see if they had seen him, but instead, I decided to go out and look for him myself.

Kilo is dead.

I felt it the minute I walked out the door. My body was numb, and my knees started shaking so hard I could barely walk. *Please God*, I prayed, *please don't take him away from me.* But I knew he was gone. I knew it even before I saw the police cars, the ambulance, or the crowd of people standing around the parking lot of the supermarket.

I didn't have to see the body underneath the white sheet to know that it was him. And, when I told the police officer that I was his next of kin, I realized that I probably was.

I asked if I could see him, and I really wasn't prepared for what I saw. He had been shot at least 5 times, and I could see the pavement through a hole where his left eye had been. The officer told me not to touch him, but I had to. I needed to feel him next to me one more time. He was covered in blood, but I didn't care, so I just lay down beside him and held him as tightly as I could. *Kilo*, I thought as I rubbed my hands all over his face and chest, *who's gonna take care of me now?*

Just then, I remembered a song my mother used to sing to me about the blood of Jesus washing away my sins. Kilo definitely wasn't Jesus; his blood probably wouldn't do a thing for me, but somehow, having his blood on my hands and face was comforting. I wanted to stay there beside him forever.

A female officer came over to me and told me that I had to get away from the body because I was contaminating evidence. We both knew there would be no investigation into Kilo's murder because everybody knew he was a pimp, so it didn't matter that he was dead. As she walked me over to her police car, I took one last glimpse over my shoulder at the man who had taken care of me for the last 3 years, and in that instant I realized that I was totally and completely alone.

5.

I had to find Jake. I didn't know what I was going to say to him when I found him, I just knew that somehow being with him would make things better. I went back to Kilo's place after he died, and that's where I stayed for a while. Apparently, he had already paid for the condo, so no one cared that I was still living there. Everything reminded me of him though, and sometimes the memories made me feel like I was suffocating, but I couldn't leave. It was our home, and I didn't want to leave the only place that made me feel safe. Kilo always kept money hidden in the bottom of a lamp that was in his bedroom. I used that money (almost $5,000) to live on until I figured out what I was going to do next.

I decided I would have a better chance of running into Jake if

I stayed close to the salon, so I rented a room at the Blake Inn across the street from Queen of the Nail. From the outside, Blake Inn looked kind of sleazy because the building had run-down steps out front, and the paint was chipping and peeling. But, once I got inside, the room was really clean. They even had coffee makers in the rooms which I thought was nice, even though I don't drink coffee. Anyway, after I unpacked and watched a little TV, I went across the street to see if Coco or anybody was there.

To my surprise, Coco was not only there, but when she came to the door, she seemed very happy to see me.

"DIVA!!" she screamed, as she gave me a big hug. "Where have you been? You know you can't go that long without getting your nails done. Let me look at your hands." Then she grabbed my hands and started feeling all over my fingers.

"Uh-huh," she said after a few minutes. "Your nails are looking too crunchy honey. Come on in here and let me take care of you right now."

So, I went.

Everything was the same as I remembered. I hadn't been there in a few months, but nothing had changed. I didn't see No Shoes and Platforms, but I knew they had been there because there were half-eaten salads sitting at their manicure stations.

"You look tired, Jem," Coco said.

"It's been a tough couple of months," I said. I wasn't in the mood to go into details about Kilo's death, but if Coco wanted to talk about it, I would. Somehow, not remembering what happened made it seem less real, but I knew I would eventually have to face the fact that Kilo was gone. Fortunately, Coco didn't press the issue. She started talking about her plans to remodel the salon. She told me they needed more space because she planned to add more manicurist's booths, as well as a small second hand clothing boutique at the back of the store.

"I've decided to call my boutique, Sophisticated Trash," she said. "I think that sounds tres funky, wouldn't you agree Jem?"

"Sure," I said, but my mind was somewhere else. I wanted--no, I needed to see Jake. Maybe he would laugh in my face or ignore me like he did the first time I saw him, but I didn't care. I needed him. I needed someone…anyone. I didn't want to talk to Coco about Kilo's death, but I did want to talk to her about the way I had been feeling lately.

It seemed as if everyone I loved was either dead, or they didn't love or want me. My mom decided it was better to kill herself rather than to deal with what was going on between me and my dad. I guess my mom had talked about what went on with some of her relatives before she died because none of them wanted anything to do with me either. Kilo loved me in his own way, but I didn't have him to depend on anymore. The only person who was still alive who claimed to love me was my father, but loving him meant losing my childhood and virginity.

Sometimes I wondered if life was worth living, if *I* was worth living. I had been thinking about killing myself a lot lately, and it kinda scared me. I needed someone to care about me. I needed someone to love me the right way. I don't know why I thought Jake could give me that kind of love, but I figured since I didn't have anything to lose, it was worth a try.

"Has Jake been around?" I asked.

"Now you want to say something," Coco said. "I've been talking to you for the last 5 minutes, and you've been staring into space like you were in some kind of trance. I should have known you were thinking about Jake. Well, honey he was in here a few days ago, and no, he didn't ask about you. As a matter of fact, he hasn't mentioned you at all since the last time."

Well, that wasn't exactly what I wanted to hear. I tried not to show my disappointment, but it was written all over my face.

"I'm sorry, Jem," Coco said,

as she reached out and gently rubbed my cheek with the back of her hand. "I didn't mean to hurt your feelings, and I know I did because you're sitting there looking like you just found you have a yeast infection. You must really miss your mother, huh?"

"What does my mom have to do with anything?" I asked.

"She has everything to do with you, Kilo, and Jake. Make the connection, honey. It's obvious you're looking for a mama, but you need to wake up and smell reality, 'cause even though Kilo could cook and stuff, he was still a thug, and even though Jake may be a woman, he ain't your mama...he's a pimp. But, if it will make you feel better, Jake has to come in tomorrow around 3 o'clock to pick up a package I have for him, so if you just *have* to see him, come back then.

Besides, I'm going to need a jackhammer to work on your fingernails, and I won't be able to get one until tomorrow anyway."

At that moment, I could have kissed her. I was finally going to see Jake again, and this time, I knew he'd notice me. *Really* notice me. Besides, I was gonna need some proof about Jake being a woman anyway. Coco probably just told me that to see how I'd react. And she was wrong; I wasn't looking for a mom 'cause the one I had didn't take care of me the way Kilo did, and the way I knew Jake could. Plus, Jake was a man. He had to be, and I was gonna give him something that would make him never want to pretend to be a woman again.

Jake

6.

"Can I pray for you?"

That's what Jake said to me when I got to the salon the next day. Not, "Hi, how are you?" or "It's good to see you again," but "Can I pray for you?" Well, I didn't know what to say, so I just nodded my head up and down and said yes.

"Father in the name of Jesus, I ask that you touch this sinner and make her whole. Wash her white as snow. Let her know, Lord, that she is a dirty whore who must turn from her wicked ways and run quickly to your throne of mercy."

I couldn't believe what was happening. There I was standing in the middle of the salon, wearing an new outfit I bought, (cause I was trying to look cute for him), and I felt like a piece of trash. Instead of trying to get to know me, Jake decided to act like Jesus and cast out my demons in front of 12 women with wet nails.

I was humiliated.

I wanted to run out of the salon, but he had such a tight hold on my forehead and back that I couldn't get away. He kept praying, chanting, and saying stuff like, "Yield, sinner," and "Satan I cast you out of this girl." After what seemed like an eternity, No Shoes appeared from out of nowhere and told Jake to stop.

"Jake, leave that child alone before you make her cry," she said. "Can't you see she doesn't think your prayer meeting act is funny?"

"Jesus cast out seven demons from Mary Magdalene," he said, as he slowly let go of my head and back. "So, why can't I cast out one from her?"

"Because," Coco yelled from across the room, "you ain't Jesus. You ain't even Jesus's cousin. In fact, you're not even in the Jesus family because, in case you have forgotten Mr. Soul Saver, you need to have a few demons cast out yourself. And anyway, the last time I checked, Jesus was perfect, and we all know that you are anything but that."

Once again, Coco had come to my rescue. If I had been smart, I would have left right then and never gone back. But I was only 15, which meant I wasn't too bright, so I stayed. I couldn't believe Jake was the same person I had met before. Not that he didn't look the same; he was still as fine as ever, but he just seemed different. His attitude was different. He didn't carry himself the same way he did when we first met. He wasn't as standoffish, but he was still weird and hard to figure out. *Maybe this is how he is with all his friends*, I thought. But then, if that's how he acted when he was trying to get to know someone, I can see why he was always alone.

That was another thing that bothered me. Every time I saw Jake, he was never with anyone else. For a pimp, he sure didn't like having any of his girls around. As a matter of fact, I never heard anybody mention where his girls were, or who they were. I was curious because although he made a fool of me once again, I still wanted to get close to him, and if being one of his girls was the way to do it, then so be it.

I decided to try to talk to him.

"Hi," I said, "my name is Jem."

"Actually, your name is

Jemimah," Jake replied. "Why do you insist upon calling yourself Jem, when Jemimah is much more unique, sophisticated, and erotic?"

I could have died. He knew my name! Not only that, but he thought it was sophisticated. I wasn't sure what he meant by it being erotic, but that had to something good too. Never in a million years would I have imagined that Jake would have taken the time to find out who I was, but I guess I made a bigger impression on him the first time we met than I thought.

"I never really liked being called Jemimah," I whispered. "My mother was the only person who ever called me that because she thought it was a beautiful name. I never liked it though. Besides, Jem is a lot easier for people to say, and I don't have to explain my real name to them."

"That's one of your many problems," he said, as he started walking towards the door. "If you had pride in who you are, you'd have an occupation that required you to be vertical at all times, instead of horizontal."

And then he left.

Once again, I felt worthless. How could a person, who was so obviously messed up himself, pass judgment on me? I may be a whore, but he's a pimp, so that really doesn't make him any better than me. In some ways, it made him worse because he was making a living off the sex of other people. At that moment, I hated Jake. I hated him for the way he made me feel, but more important, I hated him because he was right. How could I have pride in myself when the only thing I did well was give pleasure to men?

I remembered talking about that meeting I had with Jake with my pastor one night, not too long ago. Sometimes, if we need special help, Min. Aiken will hold conferences with us, so we can tell him our problems. After all this time, I was still having trouble with feeling worthless, and I couldn't get the words Jake said to me out of my head. I was trying not to use my past as an excuse for the way I was feeling, but I didn't know how I could get over feeling like I was useless.

After letting me talk and cry for a while, Min. Aiken looked at me and said, "Jem, it's okay to cry about the things that have happened to you in your past, but what you have to remember is that once you gave your heart to God, your past was forgotten. One of the hardest things for us to do sometimes is to forgive ourselves. But, if God doesn't remember the things you did, why should you?"

What he said made a lot of sense, but I still couldn't understand how God could forget all the things I had done. I mean, he saw it all, and some stuff probably shocked him a little. But then again, since God has so many people to remember, maybe it is possible for him to forget every now and then. Anyway, that wasn't my problem.

I needed to know how I could stop feeling worthless. I wanted to feel like I deserved good things. Nice things. Love. Real love, not the kind that required me to provide a service in order to get anything in return. God's love is unconditional. That's what I read in my Bible, and that's what my pastor says all the time. But God can't marry me or give me a baby, so I need to find a man who can love me unconditionally. The problem is, I don't think there is anyone who can.

7.

My last encounter with Jake left me feeling dumb and useless, but I was determined that my next meeting would be different. I was going to make sure that the next time we spoke, I would be in control of the situation, and I would leave him looking like a fool.

For 2 months I stayed at the Blake Inn, and I went to get my nails done faithfully every 2 weeks. Each time I would see Jake, but I was too embarrassed to say anything to him. Sometimes, when I would walk into the salon, he would stop what he was doing and just stare at me. I guess he knew I was a little afraid of him, even though I liked him a lot. I wondered why I even bothered with this person who obviously didn't think very much of me, but there was something that drew me to him, and no matter how I tried, I couldn't stay away.

I finally decided to say something to him, after I made up my mind to ask for the same nail polish as his. Every time I went to get my nails done, I noticed that everyone else always got colors like Pink Passion, or Boogie Down Bronze, but never Really Raspberry like Jake always did. As a matter of fact, he was the *only* person who wore that color polish. I wanted to know why it seemed like no one else was allowed to wear that color. And I wanted to know if I could be the first to try it.

So, before Coco began painting my nails one day during my appointment, and just as Jake was walking past me to go out the door, I said, (loudly enough for him to hear), "Coco, paint my nails this color," and I grabbed Jake by the hand and pointed to his nails. "I

want my nails painted Really
Raspberry."

Well, in all the time I had
known Coco, I had never seen a
time when she was silent…until
now. She was speechless. She got
this look of horror on her face like I
had just told her I was a murderer.
Then Coco opened her mouth, but
nothing came out. She kept looking
at me and then looking at Jake, and
then looking at me again. By this
time, Jake had snatched his hand
away and was glaring at me and
breathing so hard that I could feel
his breath on my cheek, even though
I was sitting down and he was
standing up. I don't know why, but
I started to laugh, and I was still
laughing when I felt someone's
hands round my throat. It took me
a minute to realize that the hands
belonged to Jake, and he was
choking me.

I stopped laughing.

Everyone in the salon looked like they want to help me, but they were afraid to do anything. I had grabbed Jake's hands to try to pull them off my neck, but he was too strong for me. Now would have been a good time for Coco to come to my rescue, but she chose that time to go to the bathroom.

I wanted to leave Jake speechless, but I didn't want him to try to kill me. What was the big deal anyway? All I asked for was some stupid nail polish and the next thing I knew, I was being strangled. And the funny thing about it was, it really didn't even hurt. I mean, his hands were tight around my neck, but it didn't feel like he was squeezing that tight. It didn't *feel* like he was squeezing that tight, but he must have been because I couldn't breathe, and I felt like I was going to pass out. When I looked up into Jake's face, he had this peaceful look on his face like choking people was something he did all the time, and it gave him comfort.

What kind of man is this? I thought. After a few seconds of struggling with him, Coco went behind him, gently placed her hand on his shoulder and said, "If you're going to kill her, could you do it outside cause murder isn't exactly good for business." If I hadn't been the one being choked, I probably would have laughed, but since Jake's hands were around my throat, I didn't think her joke was too funny.

Jake did.

At first, I couldn't tell if he was laughing or crying, but when I finally looked at him again, I could tell that he was laughing. He laughed and laughed until tears rolled down his cheeks, but he didn't let go of my neck. In fact, the harder he laughed, the tighter he squeezed me. Then, just as quickly as he had started choking me, he stopped. Everyone in the salon was silent. They were either too afraid or too nosy to move. I guess they didn't get to witness a murder, or almost murder, every day, especially not at the nail salon. Anyway, I didn't care if they said anything or not. I was just glad I wasn't left alone with Jake. Platforms and No Shoes came over to where I was sitting and gave me a glass of water and some comfort.

"I'm sorry that happened, Jem," No Shoes said. "Jake is a very complex man, and there are things about him you don't know."

"I guess somebody should have told you not to ask for his polish, though," Platforms added. "It seems like an insignificant thing, but to him, that polish-that color- is one of the most meaningful things in his life."

Now I was really confused. How could a man as handsome as Jake, spend his time worrying about nail polish? And, not just worry about it, but making sure he was the only person wearing that particular shade. It just didn't make any sense. But I didn't care about that right now. He had just tried to kill me, and I was mad. Very mad. I didn't care why he loved that color so much. All I cared about was the fact that nobody had tried to hit me or harm me in any way, since that first time with Kilo, and I was going to make sure it didn't happen again. I had taken all I was gonna take from Jake, and if it was a fight he wanted, then he was going to get one.

"Hey," I yelled, and I stood up from my chair, threw my glass of water across the room, and started walking towards the back of the salon where Jake was standing with Coco and another customer. "You see these?" I said, as I held my nails up in front of his face. "These are my nails...*MY NAILS*, and I can have them painted any color I want," I yelled.

"If I want to paint my whole body Really Raspberry," I continued, "then that's what I'll do. I don't know why you like that color so much. Maybe you're some kind of a nail polish freak who can only get off on one color. Or maybe, you're just a freak. I don't know, and I don't care. The only thing I do know is if you ever put your hands on me again, you won't have to worry about painting your nails because you'll be covered in Really Blood, from head to toe."

There, I had said it, and I felt

good. I had finally stood up to Jake, and I meant every word. I stood there in front of him waiting for him to speak.

But, he didn't.

He didn't say one word to me. He just handed me a piece of paper and walked out of the salon. After a few minutes, I decided to open the note to see what he had written.

I apologize for my behavior this afternoon. Please meet me at 7:00 tonight at 4011 Eldorado Avenue. I will be waiting, and again, I apologize.

Jake

I couldn't believe my eyes. After all this time, I was finally going to get the chance to talk to this man alone. I was excited, until I started thinking about the fact that the man who just tried to kill me, now wanted to meet with me…alone. *What if he tries to kill me again?* I thought. Jake was so hard to figure out. One minute he would act like I didn't exist, and then the next minute, he would cast out demons and then later on, try to kill me. Most people probably wouldn't have gone to his house, but I had to. And, no matter what happened, I was sure it would be a meeting neither one of us would forget.

8.

Jake was insane.

I should have known it by all the things he did before I met with him, but I guess I was in denial. After going to his house though, I *knew* he was crazy. I had a hard time finding his street because it wasn't on the bus line I normally took. Since I didn't have a license, (I was still 15, plus I didn't have a car anyway), I had to look on a map to find a street that was close to Eldorado Avenue, and not too far from the closest bus line, and then walk there.

I left my house extra early because I didn't want to be late. I kinda figured that Jake was the type who didn't like people not showing up on time, and since he already tried to kill me once, I wasn't taking any chances. On the way to his house, I kept trying to convince myself that I was doing the right thing and the he just wanted to talk and make up for what he did. I didn't want to believe that Jake would try to hurt me anymore. Besides, I had already threatened him, and even though I was mad when I did it, I couldn't kill anyone. Well, maybe my dad, but he would have deserved it. Jake hadn't done any of the things my dad had done, plus, I liked him. Still, I had the feeling that going to his place might be a mistake.

I was right.

When I finally found his house, I was so nervous that I stood outside his door 10 minutes before I rang the doorbell. From the outside, his house looked like all the other houses on the block. It was made of big stones. Not brick, but stones that were kinda pink, tan, and gray mixed together. His grass smelled like it had just been cut, and he even had a flower bed in front of his porch. The only thing different about his house was that it didn't have a mailbox in the yard. There wasn't even a mailbox, or a place to put mail next to his door. *I guess he gets his mail at the post office,* I thought, and then I rang the doorbell, stood outside, and waited.

I waited, and waited, and waited for what seemed like hours. I rang the doorbell a few more times because I thought he may have been outside or maybe even asleep and hadn't heard me the first time. Still no answer. Jake had to be home. It had taken me almost an hour to get from my place to his, and I wasn't about to turn around and go back home without talking to him. I didn't know how old Jake was, but I knew he was too old to be playing games. I was the child. If anyone should have been acting stupid, it should have been me. I wasn't sure how long I should stay because I didn't want his neighbors thinking I was trying to steal something. Besides, I knew after a while, I would look like a fool standing on his porch, especially when he obviously wasn't home.

Maybe I'm too early, I thought. But I knew I wasn't. I did leave my house early, but by the time I got across town and to his place, it was about 10 minutes til 7, and I had been on his porch ringing his doorbell at least 15 or 20 minutes. I decided to give it one more try before I left. So, I got as close to his front door as I could and said, "Jake, are you there? It's Jem. I mean Jemimah. Are you there?"

To my surprise, he answered.

"Yes, I'm here. I've been here all the time, he said, as he

opened the door.

I wanted to slap him.

How could he let me stand outside all that time and not let me in? Why would he do that? Why was he always testing me and playing stupid games? I should have turned around right then and gone back home, but I didn't. I wanted to see him. I wanted to talk to him.

"Why did you do that?" I asked, when he finally let me in the house. "I thought you weren't here. I've been here almost 30 minutes."

"I know how long you've been here, Jemimah," he said casually.

"Well, if you knew I was here," I snapped, "why didn't you come to the door?"

"'But the fruit of the Spirit is love, joy, peace, *longsuffering*, kindness, goodness, faithfulness, gentleness, *self-control.*' I really think you need to concentrate more on longsuffering and self-control, Miss Jemimah. There will be things in your life that you will need to wait longer than 30 minutes for. You need to understand that things don't, and won't always come when you want them too, even when it seems like those things are right in the palm of your hand."

Great. So now he wanted to give me a Bible lesson. His rudeness had nothing to do with me not being longsuffering or not having self-control. He was just rude, and I would have told him so, but I figured it wouldn't matter anyway. Or, he'd probably just quote a scripture on why rudeness was a virtue. Besides, I wanted to look at the rest of his house. We were standing in the living room, and even though I had seen some weird places in my life, I had never seen anything quite like this.

There had to have been at least 200 pictures of Jesus on his walls. I mean they were everywhere. There were so many pictures of Jesus all over the walls that it looked like wallpaper. Of course, it couldn't have been because I don't think Christian bookstores sell Jesus wallpaper (at least I've never seen it). Jake even had a big picture of Jesus painted on the ceiling. When I looked up, all I saw were these two big eyes staring at me. It looked like Jesus was holding a Bible, and he had a really weird look on his face. He looked like he wanted to smile, but he didn't know how, or maybe he shouldn't smile because he was Jesus and everything, and being extra holy and smiling didn't go together.

Jake took my hand and led me to a room that would have been a dining room in most people's houses, and it would have been one in his too, except the only furniture it had in it was 2 wooden chairs that were painted the same color as Jake's fingernails. As a matter of fact, when I looked at the walls, (or what I could see of them around all the Jesus pictures), I realized that they were painted Really Raspberry too.

We sat down in the chairs, and after a few minutes of silence, I blurted out, "So Jake, you really like Jesus a lot, don't you?"

He just looked at me. I didn't know what his stare meant, so I kept on talking.

"I mean, I've never seen so many pictures of Jesus in one place. Are you Catholic? I know Catholics are really supposed to like God and Mary and stuff, and umm, well, you know, if you are Catholic, I'm sure you get extra blessings or something for all your Jesus pictures."

I wished he would have said something--anything, but he didn't. At least he didn't say anything at first. Jake stared at me, and all of a sudden, I felt naked. He wasn't looking at me like he was trying to undress me, though. It wasn't that kind of stare at all. He was just looking at me like he was trying to see into my soul. Like he wanted to look through my skin and into my mind, or maybe my heart if I was lucky.

"Jemimah," he said, "do you know what the name Jacob means?"

"No," I said.

"It means deceiver. Deceiver, Jemimah. That's who I am, who *Jake* is, and that's who Jesus was. He was the biggest deceiver of them all. I'm not Catholic, Baptist, or any other religion you can think of. I

93

don't keep these pictures of Jesus around because I am 'into Jesus stuff' as you might say. I'm not into his stuff. I'm into his mind. I'm into the way he has millions believing that he is 'the way, the truth, and the light' when in actuality, he is the creator of darkness. I admire him. No, I idolize him, and that's why I surround myself with his image."

I wanted to pretend like I hadn't heard what he had just said, but I couldn't. How could Jake possibly believe Jesus was playing tricks on people? Jesus didn't do things like that, did he? When my mom used to read the Bible to me at night, she never talked about Jesus fooling people. He did perform a lot of miracles, and that was for real…wasn't it? Yeah, it was real. Jake was just confused, and he was trying to confuse me too. I had started getting a little scared, but I didn't want to leave. Not yet. I wanted to hear more, and I wanted to know why he choked me when I said I wanted my nails done like his. There was so much I wanted to know. I just hoped he would be willing to tell me.

9.

Sometimes, when I think about that first night at Jake's house, it makes me cry. I had never met a person who felt so right about doing the wrong things. I mean, he really believed all the things he told me about Jesus, and about why he decided to live his life as a man.

Jake didn't think his life was a lie. He didn't even think people should be interested in why he only got his nails painted one color, or why he wanted people to think he was a man, when supposedly he wasn't. In fact, Jake thought Jesus would be pleased at the way he was living his life. He thought God would be flattered that someone loves his son Jesus so much that he patterned his whole life after him.

Then there were the fingernails. If he wanted people to

really believe he was a man, why the nails? Why get acrylic nails, and then keep them painted bright raspberry? Didn't Jake know that would draw attention to him? Or maybe, that was what he wanted. Maybe that was how he attracted young girls like me. I didn't know how to ask him about his nails at first, so I decided that since nothing I said seemed to come out right anyway, I might as well just come right out and ask him.

"Why do you get your nails done?" I asked.

He ignored me. At least I thought he had ignored me because he didn't answer me. Well, actually, he did answer me; he just didn't answer that question.

"I don't usually invite guests into my home," he said. "You are the first houseguest I've had in a very long time. I'm a very private person, and in my line of work, it is definitely better to keep the personal and private separate."

"However," he continued, "since you and I are in the same business, I thought inviting you here might be appropriate, especially after the events that took place this afternoon. But, I still haven't decided what I want to do with you yet. You are quite beautiful, that much is true; however, in spite of your inquisitive nature, you remain ignorant. You are a peculiar treasure, Ms. Jemimah. A peculiar treasure indeed.

That was the first time anyone had called me a peculiar treasure, and the first time I had heard that expression, but it wasn't the last. A few years after Jake died, I was at church one night, when Mother Welch, one of the elderly church mothers, called me over to where she was sitting because she said she wanted to talk to me.

"I seen the way you been lookin' at that boy who plays the trumpet in the church band," she said. "But before you go gettin' all peppery in your panties, there are some things you need to know."

That *boy* she was talking about was a *man* named Kedar who played the trumpet for the church. I really didn't think anyone had been paying attention to the way I had been looking at him, but I guess I was wrong. I couldn't help it though. Kedar was the most handsome man I had seen since Jake. Kedar had smooth beautiful brown skin and curly dark hair. I didn't know if he lifted weights, but his body looked like he did, but the best part about him was his mouth. He had sexy heart shaped lips that were wrapped around the prettiest white teeth I had ever seen. I wasn't sure how it felt to be in love with someone, but I knew I could probably feel it for him. Kedar was the first man I had really been attracted to since I stopped trickin', but I had to admit that even though I only saw him at church, he didn't make me think holy thoughts.

Maybe that was it. Maybe Mother Welch saw the lusty love on my face. I guess she could tell that things might get out of hand, and that's why she needed to talk to me. Anyway, she wasn't going to let me leave until she had said everything she wanted to say, and even though I knew I wasn't going to like most of it, I listened anyway.

"Sis. Jem," she began, "I hope you know I don't mean no harm in what I'm sayin'. I'm just an old lady who's seen just about everything there is to see. Ain't nothin' none of you young girls can do that ain't been done before, and that *I* ain't done myself."

By this time, Mother Welch had taken one of my hands in hers, and she was looking at me the way my mom used to look at me after she had given me a spanking, even though she really didn't want to. It was like she was sorry for having to do what she did, but not sorry because it was for my own good. Suddenly, I felt 6 years old instead of 18.

"I know you're not trying to hurt my feelings, Mother Welch," I said. "I just don't think I've done anything wrong."

"Yet, Sis. Jem. Yet. I can tell by the way you look at him that you wish he was wrapping his lips around you instead of that horn."

I was embarrassed.

"Don't look shame now," she

101

continued. "I know where you been, Miss Jem. I know what you used to do. And I also know that God done delivered you from all that. He don't remember none of what you used to do. But the Devil, well, he ain't forgot nothin'. See, that's his job. He got to make sure he keep bringin' up stuff or puttin' thoughts in your head to keep you confused and keep you out of Heaven. Now you don't see nothin' wrong with lookin' at that boy and thinkin' bout how fine he look, but there's plenty wrong with it."

I wanted to say something, but I couldn't. I hadn't really thought about sex that much since I joined Shepherd's Fold, but I did think about it every now and then. More *now* than *then*, since Kedar joined the church, but I didn't do anything about it. I mean, I didn't try to ask him out or flirt (not that much at least). We barely spoke to each other, but I did think he kinda liked me a little because he was always smiling at me, and once he told me how pretty I looked in a dress I had worn one Sunday. That was it. It was all innocent, but Mother Welch didn't think so.

"See, Jem. The Devil starts his work with a thought. It seems like nothin' at first. A smile here, a 'how you been' there, and the next thing you know, all your clothes done fell off, and you in bed with that boy, and you don't even know how you got there. You know how old I am, Jem?"

"No ma'am."

"I'm 89 years old. 89 years I have lived in this world, and you know what? I still got all my original teeth. I don't wear no glasses, and I don't walk with no cane. You know why?

"Because you're blessed, Mother Welch. Living a long time is a blessing, isn't it?" I asked.

"Yes, it is, but that's only part of the reason I have length of years. That's what the Bible say, you know. The Lord say he'll give you length of years if you live according to his word. You'll be known as a 'peculiar treasure.' That's what the Word say. That's why I'm tellin' you all this, Jem. I want you to live your life the right way. The Lord done blessed you to get out of the situation you was in before, and now you have another chance. You have another chance to live upright and holy before the Lord, and I want you to. I want to see you do good."

I started crying before I realized it. She was right. I had been given a second chance, and I wanted to do the right thing every day. I didn't know if I would live as long as she did because I got saved later than she did, but I did know that what she was telling me was for my own good. It was just so hard though.

I know the Bible talks about not committing fornication before you are married, but how do you stop when you're so used to having it? I had been without it for a while, but it was hard for me to see somebody I thought was attractive and not *think* about it. And what about when I fell in love? What was I supposed to do then? How could I have a relationship without sex? I wanted to ask Mother Welch all of these questions, but it was already late, and I could tell she was tired, and so was I.

Instead, I just gave her a big hug and thanked her for talking to me. I told her I was still struggling with the whole sex thing, but I would pray every time I got the urge. And as long as Kedar was around, I knew I was going to be spending a lot of time at the altar.

10.

Mother Welch died a few months after her 90th birthday, and I've often thought about the words she said to me, especially the "peculiar treasure," because that reminded me of Jake.

That night I went to his house changed my life. I learned things about him, and myself that have stayed with me in the years since his death. I really didn't think he would answer all the questions I had for him, but he did. In his own time, and in his own way, he answered them all.

"What does being a peculiar treasure have to do with your fingernails?" I asked.

"It has everything to do with them, Jemimah. As I stated earlier, your inquisitive nature has still left you in a state of ignorance. In your case, however, I think ignorance suits you well."

"What's that supposed to mean, Jake?" I said. "Yeah, I know you think I'm stupid. You think I don't know much about anything. Well, you're wrong. I know a lot of things. I may only be 15, but I've done some things in my life, and I've had to think for myself for a long time. I'm not as dumb as you think."

"I don't recall ever saying you were dumb, Jemimah," he said. "I just merely stated that your lack of knowledge concerning my personal business suits you well. If I offended you by using the word 'ignorance,' I apologize. I meant no harm."

One of the things I hated about Jake was his ability to say rude and nasty things and then act like I just took it the wrong way. He almost made *me* want to apologize because *he* called me ignorant.

"Jake, I'm just tired of the way you make me feel. You act like you don't mean to put me down or make me feel dumb, but I think you do. You think that because I'm a prostitute, I don't have feelings. Maybe the girls who work for you don't feel anything or don't care about anything, but I'm not like that. I'm not like that at all."

I was going to cry, and I didn't want to. I didn't want him to see how hurt I was. I didn't want him to know that all I wanted was to be close to him, and the more he pushed me away, the more I needed him. I didn't even know why his acceptance was so important to me; I just knew I had to have it. I needed to be just as important to him, as he was to me.

As hard as I tried to fight back tears, I couldn't, and I ended up crying anyway. To my surprise, Jake came over and started rubbing my shoulders. He was close enough to me to hug me, but he didn't. He just stood in front of me rubbing my shoulders and looking at me like he was trying to decide if he should kiss me or not.

He didn't.

Instead, he sat me back down in one of the wooden chairs while he went back into the kitchen. When he came out of the kitchen, he was holding a tray that was covered with a white cloth.

"Before I tell you anything, you must purify yourself, Jemimah. We must partake of the Lord's Supper."

Well, back then, I wasn't going to church, so I didn't know

what the Lord's Supper was. I didn't even know Jesus ate dinner, but if eating Jesus's food was going to make him happy, then so be it.

"Fine," I said. "Let's eat."

He pulled the cloth off the tray, and to my surprise, all he had was some flat white crackers and a bottle of wine.

"That's it?" I asked. "I thought we were gonna have the Lord's Supper. This is just crackers, and I don't think Jesus drank alcohol."

Jake started laughing. He laughed and laughed the same way he did when he tried to choke me. This time though, it seemed like he was laughing *at* me, and I didn't like that. I wanted him to stop laughing and tell me what I had said that was so funny. If that was the only stuff Jesus ate, I didn't know it, and me not knowing something like that wasn't really very funny. I'm sure I'm not the only person who thought the Son of God would be able to eat something more than crackers and wine. The stories my mom used to read to me from the Bible didn't mention anything about the stuff Jesus ate.

"Jake," I pleaded, as the tears started again, "please stop laughing at me. I can't help it if I don't know what Jesus ate. I don't know the Bible the way you do, but I want to. I want to know everything about God like you do, so please don't laugh at me."

He stopped laughing.

For the first time since I'd met him, I thought I had said something that he wanted to hear. But, I wasn't just sayin' it, though; I really did want to know everything he knew. I wanted to know

everything about him, and I would
stay there as long as I had to until I
learned it.

"Forgive me, Jemimah," he
said with sincerity. "I often forget
that not everyone has had the
privilege of being as well versed and
well informed about the Bible as I
have. I have overlooked the fact
that you are a young girl who has
spent a great deal of time on the
streets. Therefore, studying the
Bible wouldn't be one of your top
priorities. I did, however, take it for
granted that you understood the
significance of the Lord's Supper
and what the crackers and wine
represent. I do apologize."

Then, Jake explained
everything to me. After I
understood about the body and the
blood, I felt good about taking
communion. It was my first time,
and I was glad I did it with him. I

didn't want to tell him that I had never had wine before because I knew how important it was to him and to communion. Besides, I don't think it mattered much anyway because he didn't give me enough to get me drunk.

After we took communion, he took me into another room in his house that was completely dark…at first. When we walked into the room, I expected him to turn on the lights because we couldn't see. Instead, he led me over to a chair that felt like it was metal or something because when I sat down it felt hard, and it was cold against my legs. He sat across from me, but I didn't know that until he started talking because I couldn't see him. I told him that I felt a little uncomfortable, and he assured me that in a little while I would feel better. He wanted me to just sit for a moment and "appreciate the darkness."

"Many people associate darkness with evil," he said. "But, without darkness, one cannot experience the light. You must pass through the darkness on your journey to enlightenment, Jemimah."

I was still scared.

I wasn't sure if it was the darkness that was scaring me or if it was the fact that I was sitting in the dark with someone who had tried to kill me. I still hadn't forgotten about what had happened earlier in the day, and even though things seemed to be okay now, Jake was still unpredictable. I just hoped it wasn't some kind of trick.

"I'm not going to hurt you," he said, and I wondered if he could read minds too.

"I didn't think you would," I lied. "I'm just not used to sitting in the dark."

"Relax, Jemimah.   Relax," he said.

So, I did.

After about 30 minutes or so, Jake began to talk, and he didn't stop talking until 3 hours later.

"I am aware of the fact that you wish for me to be your employer. You want to work for me because you want to be close to me. It's no secret that you are attracted to me, Jemimah, and you have every reason to be. I'm a successful businessman, although some might find my business dealings to be questionable, and I'm also quite handsome."

And conceited, I thought.

"However, please do not confuse my confidence with conceit."

How does he do that?

"I am not conceited, Jemimah. I'm convinced. I'm convinced that I am the type of person most people wish they could be. I'm convinced that if given the opportunity, most people would gladly trade places with me, if only for one day. And it is because of this that I am convinced that my intelligence far surpasses that of most."

I had to admit, Jake was pretty smart, but it seemed like he only knew Bible stuff. I hadn't heard him talk about other things, you know like politics or the economy, but then I guess he wouldn't want to discuss anything like that with a 15 year old prostitute.

"You see, Jemimah, most people covet the things or attributes of others because they haven't realized that they may already possess, or have the potential to possess the same things themselves. A man might look at me and think I epitomize the word 'man,' when in actuality, I do not. However, that same man might spend days, weeks, even years trying to emulate something that is false. Sad, isn't it?"

I wasn't sure if I was supposed to answer that question, so I didn't say anything.

"That realization gives me great pleasure, Jemimah because it lets me know I am doing my job well. It lets me know I have mastered the art of deception, and I am very pleased. Very pleased indeed."

I really wasn't sure what he was talking about, but I didn't want to interrupt. Something about the sound of his voice made me think he was smiling, which sent chills up my spine. How could anyone get pleasure out of fooling people? Why? I was trying to understand the things Jake did, but it was hard. One thing I did understand, though was that if Jake said he could fool men, then he really was a woman. And that made me very sad. Very sad indeed.

11.

"So you really are a woman?" I asked.

I could feel Jake staring at me in the darkness. At that moment, I wished I hadn't spoken, but it was too late now. I wanted to run, but I was too afraid to move. So, I sat, and I waited.

"That depends on what your definition of a woman is," he said.

"How many definitions are there, Jake? I mean, there's just men and women, and if you're not a man, then you're a woman."

"Anatomically speaking that may be true, Jemimah, but does having a vagina and breasts make you a woman?"

"It doesn't make you a man," I snapped. I really wasn't trying to be rude, (well, actually I was), but I was getting a little sick and tired of Jake. First, he had me sitting in the dark on a hard chair, and now he wanted to tell me that there were different types of women. He wasn't as smart as he thought if he didn't even know what made a man a man and a woman a woman.

"I can understand why someone like you would equate your womanhood with your vagina and breasts, especially given your line of work. Unfortunately, my dear, most women think like you think. They believe there is a direct correlation between womanhood and D-cups. The larger the breasts, the more sensual and seductive the woman. However, I have had no problem dating men, or women for that matter, without the aid of my breasts. 'We have a little sister, and she has no breasts,' Song of Solomon 8:8. They were talking about the Shulamite woman whom Solomon loved and who was very beautiful…sans breasts."

"But didn't Solomon date everybody? He loved women…all women. Besides, Coco said the Shulamite woman was crazy, and I thought Solomon said she had breasts like sheep or goats or something."

"Fawns. He said her 2 breasts were like fawns feeding among the lilies. Quite poetic. However, that was an illusion. She admits she had no breasts, but in his eyes, her breasts were like towers. In other words, his love for he made even her lack seem plentiful."

Okay, I kinda understood what he was saying, but I still didn't understand why Jake didn't want, or *have* any breasts for that matter. Was he born flat-chested, or did he have an operation? And if he didn't want to be feminine, then why the fingernails? I still wanted to know the answers to those questions.

"So, did you just wake up one day and say, 'I think I want to be a man'?"

"I was destined to be a man, Jemimah. I couldn't possibly do the things that Jesus did as a woman. Living my life in his image was what I was called to do. I didn't have a choice."

I always thought everyone had a choice in what they did in life. Even I had a choice, and my life was terrible. I could have stayed in the house with my dad and continued to let him molest me, but I chose to leave. Some may say I *had* to leave, but it was still my choice. Just like my mother chose to stay, at least until I was gone, and just like my dad chose to do the things he did. Jake wasn't any more destined to be a man, as I was destined to turn tricks.

But I didn't say anything, though. I knew he would have just said I was being ignorant, or something like that, so I just kept my thoughts in my head. Besides, I wanted him to keep telling me about his life.

"Jacob. Jake... that's who I was destined to become. The great deceiver. Are you familiar with the story of Jacob and Esau in the Bible, Jemimah?"

"Kinda," I said. "Didn't he have a twin brother who was hairy or something like that? And didn't he steal from him?"

"My earlier assumption that you knew nothing about the scriptures was wrong. Once again, I apologize. You are quite correct, Miss Jemimah. Jacob and Esau were twins, and Esau was covered with hair. Red hair to be exact. Before their father died, Jacob covered himself in sheep's hair, went in to where his father lay dying, and basically stole his brother's inheritance, or blessing."

"How come his dad didn't know who he was?"

"Because he was blind. At any rate, as a child, I was fascinated with that story. The thought of being able to pretend to be someone I was not and walk away with the blessings of God intrigued me. What intrigued me even more was the fact that God knew what was happening. He knew from the beginning that Jacob was the one called to lead and not Esau. Esau was a great man in his own right, but he did not possess the greatness that Jacob possessed. Jacob was the chosen twin, just as I was the chosen twin in my family."

Oh my God! They're 2 of them?!

"You have a twin?" I asked. "Where is he?"

"She," he corrected. "And she is dead."

I wanted to know how she died, but I thought asking him about it might be rude. Still, the curiosity was killing me. We sat there in silence for a few minutes, and I could tell that he was waiting for me to ask a question.

So, I did.

"I know I probably shouldn't ask you this," I said slowly, "but since you've decided to tell me about your life and your sister is a part of it, I guess it's okay to ask. But you don't have to answer if you don't want to. Umm, if you don't mind, would you tell me how your sister died?"

"I don't mind telling you at all, Jemimah," Jake said, and I could tell by the sound of his voice that he was standing up. I heard the click of his heels on the floor as he walked across the room, and just as he turned on a little lamp so that I was finally able to see, he looked at me and said, "I killed her. I killed my sister, Jemimah."

Of course, I thought he was kidding. I had seen spooky movies before, and I knew that he was just trying to scare me. He didn't kill his sister. He couldn't have done that. He wasn't that type. Sure, he had tried to strangle me, but I don't think he would have killed me. He was probably trying to get some kind of reaction out of me, which is why I just sat there. I didn't look scared at all either. I just sat there looking at him.

"You didn't kill your sister," I

finally said. "You're not a murderer."

"Are you forgetting what took place this afternoon in the salon?" he asked, as he walked back over to his chair and sat down.

Of course I hadn't forgotten. How could I forget someone trying to kill me? I still didn't think he was a murderer, though. He was too good-looking to be a killer. Most killers I saw were raggedy looking. Besides, killing isn't something Jesus would do, so Jake wouldn't do it either.

"No, I didn't forget what happened, but you *didn't* kill me, and I'm not even related to you. You couldn't have killed your sister, especially not your twin sister because twins are supposed to have a bond or something like that, so killing her would be like killing yourself."

"There are many ways to kill a person, Jemimah. Many ways indeed. I've said all I wish to say tonight, so if you'll excuse me, I think I'm going to retire for the evening. I'll see you to the door, and if you wish, you may return in one week, at which time, we will continue this conversation."

And that was it.

He ended the conversation just like that. I was going to have to wait a whole week before I could talk to him again. I started to tell him that I wasn't leaving, but since I was in his house, and I did want to hear the rest of the story, I decided not to say anything. So, I left, and as I sat on the bus on my way back home, I thought about my own destiny, and even though I wasn't sure what it was, I was certain that Jake was going to be a part of it.

geveryl

Ground

12.

There's a murderer at my church. Well, I guess you would call him an ex-murderer because he doesn't kill people anymore. He went to prison for killing a man over a piece of chicken. At the time, he was on drugs, and he said that *that* particular piece of chicken was the only thing he would have had to eat in about a week. The drugs made him do it.

According to him, the drugs made him do everything, which is how he ended up in jail. Drugs must really be powerful too because there's even an ex-pastor at my church who went to jail because he was "selling crack for Jesus," as he put it. He said he was just trying to help with the building fund, but the police didn't believe him, so they locked him up.

Anyway, Brother Thomas, the murderer, hadn't told anyone that he had killed another person. I don't even think Min. Aiken knew about that because he looked just as surprised as everyone else when Bro. Thomas revealed that secret in service one night.

"This is my first time getting up to testify," Bro. Thomas began. "But, the Lord has been dealing with my heart to share something with the congregation, so I gotta say what's on my mind."

No one in the church said anything because I think most of us were a little shocked that he had gotten up to speak. Even though he had been going to Shepherd's Fold about 6 or 7 months, Bro. Thomas hardly said anything to anybody…ever. He was probably one of the quietest people I had ever met. Of course, he would smile and say hello if you spoke to him, but other than that, he didn't say a word.

So, even the people who usually say, "Amen," or "Tell of his goodness," when people are testifying kept quiet so Bro. Thomas could have the floor all to himself to speak his mind.

"I don't like to talk much because I was always told that if you don't have anything to add to a conversation, then don't take anything away from it by saying something dumb," he said. "I've listened to the testimonies of different ones in the church, and I have oftentimes wanted to say something, but I guess the timing wasn't right. But lately, the Lord has been telling me to get something off my chest, so to speak. I'm asking that you all remember that we are all God's children, and that when we became members of the family of

God, all our past sins were washed away and thrown into the sea of forgetfulness."

Bro. Thomas had more to say, but he had to stop talking for a minute because he was crying. I could hear several members of the church sniffling and blowing their noses too, and I almost started crying myself. Everyone could see that he was carrying a huge burden, and we all wanted to help him. We all wanted him to know that he wasn't the only one with secrets or shame.

"I killed a man," he said suddenly. "I killed a man, and I went to prison for 25 years. For 25 years, I saw that man's face every morning, noon, and night. For 25 years, I told that man I was sorry for what I had done. 25 years, Saints. 25 years. I took his life over some food. Not even *some* food…one piece. Just one piece of cold chicken that I never ate anyway," and then he started crying again.

By this time, most of us were in tears too. Nobody at the church had committed normal sins. I mean, everybody seemed to have done things that most people don't do. So, it didn't really matter why he had gone to jail, at least not to most of us. I'm sure there were a few who might have been afraid of him at first, but not for long.

"All those years in prison, I didn't know nothing about the Lord. I didn't know that there was someone who would forgive me and help me forgive myself for what I had done. So, for 25 years, I hated. I hated everything and everybody because I didn't know where to find love. I didn't know I could. But brothers and sisters, let me tell you, one day I met a man, and his name was Jesus. I was walking down the street one day, and I met a street preacher by the name of Min. Aiken, and he asked me if he could introduce me to me to his friend."

"Of course," Bro. Thomas continued, "I thought he was talking about one of his buddies, you know, another guy, but then he started telling me about Jesus and his mercy and grace. He told me that I could have a clean slate. That if I gave my heart to the Lord, everything I had ever done would be washed away. Well, at that point in my life, I didn't have anything to lose, so I said, 'Mister, if you know a man like that, I sure want to meet him.' And meet him I did. Saints, I want to tell you tonight that when I asked the Lord to forgive my sins and come into my heart, something inside me just exploded. I felt like one of those rockets, except I wasn't going to the moon. No sir, I was going straight from the ground to God."

After Bro. Thomas's testimony, people in the church clapped, yelled, "Hallelujah," and shouted around the church for at least 30 minutes. The way he said he felt was the same way most of us felt, but no one had ever put in words like that before.

At first, I was happy too, but then I started thinking about Jake, and I realized that he probably never had that rocket feeling. He didn't get the chance to feel the way we felt. In his mind, he was already doing the Lord's work. He was already Jesus the 2nd, so he really didn't need to repent of anything. He'd rather kill himself than admit he was wrong or that *he* needed God. And, he did. He killed himself, and I was the one he had chosen to be with him when he did it.

13.

I thought I was gonna die.

That week between the time Jake and I first spoke at his house, and the time we would talk again seemed like the longest week in my life. I had only turned a few tricks that week because I couldn't concentrate on anything except our conversation. Besides, I was beginning to really get tired of what I was doing. The problem was, I was 16 (my birthday was the day after I went to Jake's house), and I didn't know how to do anything else. Turning tricks didn't leave me with many job options.

Anyway, I did go get my nails done because they looked bad. I never got them painted the last time I was there because Jake started choking me before I had the chance. Plus, I was hoping I might run into him while I was there.

I didn't.

Coco was happy to see me, though. She said she was a little surprised that I came back so soon, especially after what had happened the last time I was there.

"Jemimah," she said, as she gave me a big hug, "I didn't know if you were ever going to come back."

"I needed to get my nails done," I said.

"I can see that honey, but since murder and manicures don't mix well together, I just assumed you would stay away. I don't know what gets into Jake sometimes. Most of the time, he is so sweet and calm, but then sometimes he just goes crazy. It's like he snaps or something. Yes, honey; he definitely has a Jevil thing going on."

I gave her a strange look because I didn't know what a Jevil was, and she started to laugh.

"Jesus mixed with the devil. Jevil. I made that up, and I think it's rather original, if I do say so myself. But, you know mixing Jesus with the devil is like mixing cramps with the flu…it ain't cute. Speaking of not being mixed together right, how was your meeting with Jake?"

How did she know I had seen him? I thought.

"You don't have to look so shocked," she laughed. "I was with him when he wrote you the note, remember? So, did he show you his preserves?"

"We didn't talk about food," I said.

Coco just gave me a blank stare, and then she started to smile.

"Baby, this is Jake we are talking about. I'm not talking about food either. But, since you don't know what I mean, he must not have gotten that far yet. 'Cause trust me Jem, if you had seen Jake's preserves, you would remember."

Well, I was going back to his house the next day, so I didn't have long to wait to see his preserves. I wanted to ask her how many times she had been to Jake's house, or if she knew how many other girls had been there, but I didn't. I just sat still and let her paint my fingernails.

When she got finished, I told her that I probably wouldn't be back for a while. I don't know why I said it, but I just felt like after my talk with Jake the next day, I may not want to get my nails done anymore. I've never been psychic or anything, but I just had a very strange feeling about tomorrow.

"You may not be back to get your nails done, Jem," Coco said, as she walked me to the door, "but you will be back. You will be back."

14.

I saw my father on the way to
Jake's house. I almost didn't
recognize him because it had been 4
years since the last time we saw each
other. I had just gotten off the bus
and was walking down the street
towards Jake's house, when I saw
him coming out of a coffee shop. It
was kinda funny too because when I
was at home, I never remembered
my dad drinking coffee before, but
there he was with a coffee cup in
one hand and a donut in the other.

He looked old.

I didn't know what his real
age was, but I knew it couldn't have
been as old as he looked. His hair
was almost completely white, and he
had huge bags and dark circles under
his eyes. He looked like he cried all
the time. He still had his fat
stomach, though. He didn't see me,

so I followed him. I don't know why I did that. I guess I just wanted to know where he was going. Our house wasn't in this neighborhood, so he couldn't have been going home.

Maybe he moved. I thought. He could have moved, seeing how nothing good happened where we lived. I really should have been on my way to Jake's because I didn't want to be late, but I had to see what my dad was doing. A part of me wanted to say something to him. I wondered if he ever thought about what happened. Did he miss me? Did he even care that I was gone? What did he do after mom died? I wanted him to see that all those years of abuse hadn't killed me. I wanted him to see that I was doing okay, and that I didn't need him to survive. I wanted to spit in his face and tell him that if it hadn't been for him, my mother would still be alive.

I wished he had blown his brains out instead of her. I wanted him to be dead. I had so many questions that I knew would never be answered because I didn't say anything to him. I stopped following him and just stood on the corner watching him walk farther and farther away from me.

When my dad was completely out of sight, I turned around and ran to Jake's house as fast as I could. I knew I was going to be late, and I just hoped and prayed that he would let me in. To my surprise, when I got there, he was sitting on his porch reading a book. As I got closer, I saw that the book was the Bible.

"I'm sorry I'm late," I said, "but I kinda ran into someone I hadn't seen in a long time. Are you mad?"

He didn't say anything. He just kept on reading like he hadn't heard a word I said.

"Jake, I said I'm sorry. Is everyth-"

"Let's go inside," he interrupted. And then he closed the Bible, got up, and went into the house.

I followed him.

When we got inside, he slammed the door real hard and grabbed me by the back of my neck. I wanted to scream. Actually, I *did* scream, but no sound came out because I was so scared that all I could manage to get out was a little whimper.

"Harsh discipline is for him who forsakes the way, and he who hates correction will die!" he yelled, as he pulled me towards the kitchen. I felt my knees get weak, and I thought I was going to fall, but I didn't.

"Jemimah, 'He who spares his rod hates his son, but he who loves him disciplines him promptly.' That's in the Bible, and it's in there for a reason. You obviously weren't taught the meaning of punctuality, or the significance of obeying those who have rule over you. You were supposed to be here at 7:00. 7:00 Jemimah, not 7:01, 7:03 or 7:04. My time is precious. Do you think I don't have anything better to do than to sit around and wait for you? Do you?"

By this time, he was yelling in my face. I mean, he had his face about 1 inch away from mine, and he was holding me by the back of my head. I was standing up against the refrigerator, and I was shaking so hard that I could hear the bottles inside the refrigerator rattling.

"JJJake," I stammered, "please don't hurt me. I'm really sorry, and I wasn't trying to be late. I, umm, well the bus, it just was a little off schedule, and I couldn't help it."

"Buy the truth, and do not sell it, Miss Jemimah," he said. He let go of my head and walked over to one of the cabinets above the stove and pulled out an extension cord.

"'Do not withhold correction from a child, for if you beat him with a rod, he will not die. You shall beat him with a rod, and deliver his soul from hell.' That's Proverbs 23:13. So you see Jemimah, it's not me who believes you should be chastised for your disobedience, it's God. I didn't make the rules; God did, and since his spirit lives in me, I must do as I am commanded, or else I will suffer the consequences. Please understand, Jemimah," he said as he slowly walked over to where I was shaking in front of the refrigerator.

"If I didn't love you, I wouldn't do this to you. But, like the Bible says, it won't kill you; it will only deliver you from Hell."

I didn't remember anything after that because I passed out. When I woke up, I was lying in a bed underneath a blanket that was covered with rose petals. I didn't think they were real at first, but when I touched one of them, I found out that they were. I was also in a lot of pain. It was hard for me to move my arms and legs, and when I finally managed to lift one of my arms up from under the blanket, I saw that it was covered with deep red welts.

"Don't you love the smell of roses?" Jake asked.

I hadn't even noticed he was there, but when I turned my head, I saw that he was sitting across the room in what looked like a rocking chair. I also noticed that the room I was in didn't have as many pictures of Jesus on the walls as the others. As a matter of fact, there were only 1 or 2 really big pictures of him on the walls. The rest of the room was painted purple and red, and I saw pictures of people, (real people, not Jesus), on a frame on the dresser.

"I hurt. I hurt all over," I said after a few minutes.

"I know you do, but sometimes the best love comes with pain. You'll feel better soon. I'll bring you something to drink in the meantime," he said, and then he left.

When he came back, he was carrying the same tray he had when we took communion, only this time, it wasn't covered with a white cloth. There was a pitcher on the tray, and it had some kind of pinkish purplish liquid in it. I didn't want to drink it.

"What kind of juice is this?" I asked.

"It's a combination of grape juice and grapefruit juice," he said. "I used to drink it all the time when I was a child. It may sound a little distasteful, but it is rather delicious. Please try it."

So, I did.

To my surprise, it was kinda good. Or, maybe I was just thirsty. At any rate, I drank a couple of glasses of it. I told him it was good, and he seemed pleased that I liked it. He went over to the chair where he had been sitting and pulled it up close to the bed.

"It's time we continued our conversation from last week," he began. "I would appreciate it if you would limit your interruptions."

I didn't say a word.

"Good. I know you had every intention of working for me; however, I am particular about who I induct into my 'family' so to speak. My girls aren't like the other girls one might normally find on the streets. Each of my girls is special. Each has a gift or talent that is useful to me."

He paused, and I almost asked him a question…almost. I realized that he was probably testing me to see if I would disobey his instructions, so instead of asking him what he meant by talents that were useful to him, I kept my mouth shut.

"You remind me of my sister. She was the oldest by 30 seconds, and she acted as though she were older by 30 years. I remember when we were little, she used to always want to give me instructions. If we were going to play a game, she always made up the rules, and if by some chance I was winning, she would change them."

He was smiling, and I could tell that his sister was someone who was very special to him. It was hard for me to picture Jake as a child because he was always so serious. But, he was a lot older now than he was then, so I guess things were different.

"My home life was a lot like yours Jemimah." He must have seen the shocked expression on my face and the question in my eyes because he started to laugh. "I've been around a long time, and I've met many, many girls just like you. You wear your Purple Heart of abuse on your sleeve. But I understand. I understand."

I wasn't sure how much longer I could keep quiet. At that moment, I wanted to talk to him about the things that had happened to me as a child. I wanted to tell him that it was my father I had seen today and not the bus being off schedule. I wanted to ask him if it was wrong of me to just let him walk away without saying a word. I wanted to…but I didn't. I just looked at him and tried my best to keep from crying.

"My sister left home when we were 13. She thought that at 13 years of age, she could secure employment and then come back home and rescue me. Well, she did find a job. The only job a 13 year old could get making enough money to support two people. After she would meet her johns at night, she would sneak into my room and we'd talk for hours. She had started wearing make-up because she had to look older than she was; otherwise, she wouldn't have had much business"

Jake paused for a moment and let out a sigh.

"I missed her terribly, so when she would come over at night to cheer me up, she would put make-up on my face and paint my nails the same color as hers. Really Raspberry. That was the color of the nail polish she always wore. She used to buy it at the corner drug store. I think back then, it only cost about 50 cents a bottle. I thought it was very bright, especially for someone as young as we were, but she told me that it attracted men, so that's why she wore it."

So that was it. Because of his sister, that was the reason he got his nails painted that color. I felt sorry for him. I never had any brothers or sisters, but I always wished I did. I knew there was some kind of connection between me and Jake, though. He had the same life I had, and that's why I was so drawn to him. But, if he loved his sister so much, and he didn't like what she was doing, why did he become a pimp? And, why did he say he killed her? I opened my mouth to speak, but the look in his eyes told me that I better not. Instead, I pointed to the pitcher of juice, and he poured me a glass full.

"I would probably still be a virgin if it hadn't been for my father," he continued. "Sex is highly overrated. In fact, my sister used to tell me how much she hated having sex with all those men. 'They always smell like beer and sweat,' she used to say. And, most of them were old enough to be her father. Still, she did what she had to do…for me. After she started developing breasts, however, she had more customers, so she wasn't able to see me every night like she used to. But, she would call when our dad wasn't at home, just to make sure I was doing well."

Jake looked like he was going to cry, and I prayed that he wouldn't. I could tell that he was having a hard time telling me this story, and I wondered why he decided to open up to me in this way.

Little did I know, I was about to find out.

15.

Thinking about that night makes me very sad. I had a chance to tell Kedar about it one day (yes, we did end up talking, and that's all). He was really a very smart guy who got caught up with drugs because of music. Kedar said everybody always told him that he was a musical genius. A super genius, if there is such a thing. The only problem was, his records weren't selling. People liked his stuff, but they wouldn't even play it on the radio stations in his hometown. It made him crazy, and it hurt him a lot.

"Jem, the drugs were my means of escape," he said. "See, when I was high, it didn't matter that no one was supporting what I was trying to do. It didn't matter that I had been playing all my life, and although some of the best musicians in the world were groovin' to my

music, I still couldn't get any airplay.
Nothing mattered but the drugs."

Well, of course he was so into
drugs that he stopped playing music
completely. Actually, he couldn't
play anymore because he was so
high. Eventually, Kedar got his life
together, though, and after meeting
Min. Aiken and joining the church,
he started playing for the church.

Anyway, when we were
talking about Jake, I told him that
even though I was in a lot of
physical pain that day, I could tell
Jake's pain was a lot worse. Kedar
didn't think he was in pain, though.
He just thought Jake was crazy and
should have been in an institution.

"How can you feel sorry for
someone who nearly beat you to
death?" he asked. "And, it's not like
you didn't know he was capable of
violence because he had choked you
the week before. And I'm not even

going to get into the whole *him* really being a *her* thing. You're blessed to have gotten out of there alive."

And, I was.

Jake told me that his sister had gotten turned on to drugs by one of the girls she worked with. It was harmless at first; you know, just a little marijuana, but then she started shooting heroin. Eventually, she stopped coming over to the house altogether, and that's when he started going out at night to look for her.

"It didn't dawn on me that people would get the 2 of us confused," he told me. "I had almost forgotten that we were identical twins because she looked so different, at least to me. Her johns, on the other hand, thought I was her. They thought she had gotten off the drugs and was back to her old self. I couldn't believe the conditions in which my sister lived. I couldn't believe the extent of her love for me either. She was willing to suffer through the sexual abuse of numerous men, just so I could have a better life, without any thought of her own safety. It was truly unconditional love."

This time, he did start to cry, and so did I. I wanted to reach out and touch him, but I was still in a lot of pain. So instead, I just put my hand over one of his hands that was resting on my blanket, and I lightly rubbed my fingers over his.

"I finally found my sister," he said, after he had gotten himself together. "She was lying under a pile of trash in an alley. One of the drunks who was living on the street saw me and said, 'Hey, I thought I saw you over there a few minutes ago,' and he pointed to an alley across the street. 'You didn't look like you was in no condition to walk. How'd you do that'?"

By the time he got to his sister, she was dead.

"I remember brushing the trash out of her hair and off her clothes and holding her close to me. I tried to breathe into her mouth because I thought that since we were twins, my breath would give her life, but it didn't. She was covered in dirt from head to toe, and when I looked down, all I saw were those bright nails shining through the darkness. It was at that moment that my life changed forever, and I realized what I must do."

I could tell it was getting late, and I wanted to go home, but I couldn't move. My body was still hurting, and to be honest, I wasn't sure if I *could* move. Jake told me to stay there for the night, and we would continue the conversation in the morning, so I did.

I didn't get much sleep, though. I couldn't. I kept thinking about everything he had told me, and I knew that there was more to come…much more. The only problem was, I wasn't sure I wanted to hear it.

16.

The next morning, Jake cooked me breakfast. I woke up to the smell of eggs and bacon, and it made me miss Kilo terribly. No one had cooked for me since he died, and I had forgotten how special those times were for me. I was sure Jake knew all about Kilo because they were both pimps. I didn't think there was a pimp club or anything like that; it's just that they had to know about each other so they could stay away from each other's girls and territories. Besides, I had heard from several Strawberries (those were the really pretty girls who got passed along from one drug dealer to the next), that all the pimps and drug dealers at least knew *of* each other.

Anyway, when Jake brought me the food, I almost inhaled it because I was so hungry. I realized, after I had started eating, that I hadn't eaten anything in 2 days. Jake didn't eat anything, though. He just sat beside the bed and watched me.

"Have you ever noticed that men seem to have all the true power?" he asked suddenly. "After my sister's death, I realized that the only power women seemed to possess was between their legs or on their chest. Delilah, Jezebel, Herodias were all responsible for the downfall or death of 'Men of God' and they all used their bodies to do it. But afterwards, they were cast aside or killed. They were only good for one thing. But the men? Well, the men who survived still got to serve God and do great things. They were still great!"

Jake was yelling at this point, but I don't think he knew it. He had gotten himself really worked up by this time, and I was afraid. Things had changed since yesterday, and I was more frightened of him now than I had ever been. I noticed that he had changed his way of talking. When I first met him, he used big words that I didn't know the meaning of, but as time went on, he started using words I could understand, and sometimes he didn't even make sense at all. But, I didn't say anything. I just let him talk.

"Men can use women and discard them without any remorse," he said. "And, they can't do a thing about it. I knew I had to do something. I knew I had to make a change."

That's when he told me he decided to become a man, or at least look like one. He said the only way he could try to make sense of what happened, not only to his sister, but also to him, was to do like Jesus did.

"The great deceiver, Jemimah.

All those Bible stories my father read to me right after he would have sex with me, flooded my mind. All those scriptures about how Jesus loved me and cared about me and everyone in the world. Yet, *He* allowed my father to molest me, and *He* allowed my sister to sell her body and eventually die because *He* didn't provide a way out. The only person who showed me unconditional love was my sister...not *Him*. Not God. Yet, people still believe. I wanted people to believe in me the same way, especially men. They're really quite moronic, you know."

Well, I didn't know because I didn't know what "moronic" meant. I just knew it wasn't anything good. The only thing I did know was that I wanted to get out of there. Jake was obviously insane, and I didn't need to stick around any longer to figure that out. Unfortunately, I wasn't feeling any better from the beating I had gotten the day before, so I was stuck.

I asked him if I could go to the bathroom, and he said he'd help me in a few minutes. I didn't know why he couldn't help me then, but I didn't bother to ask.

Eventually, he did help me out of the bed and into the bathroom, but he didn't leave me alone. I guess he thought I might try to escape if I had the chance, so he stayed there in the bathroom with me while I used the toilet.

"I'm not used to peeing with people around," I said, quite innocently.

"Must you always use such vulgar language, Jemimah," he snapped. "Since you're a hooker, you are disqualified from the 'young lady' category; however, you could still have some manners in the presence of your elders."

Now he was talking like the old Jake I knew. But, the old Jake was the one who choked me and beat me with an extension cord. I didn't like him. I didn't like that Jake at all.

Since I was in the bathroom, and he wasn't telling me his story anymore, I decided that it would be a good time to ask questions. He shouldn't get mad because I wasn't interrupting. So, while I was washing my hands, I asked Jake if it was hard going from a woman to a man since he was so young.

Jake looked at me like he had hoped I would ask that question, and he was more than happy to tell me all the details.

After hearing his response, however, I wished I had never asked that question.

"Wearing men's clothing wasn't difficult because I was a tomboy growing up, so I had nothing but trousers in my wardrobe," he explained. "The only time I wore make-up was when my sister would put it on me, so that was no problem either. The only obstacles in my way were my breasts. I could not possibly afford an operation, especially at such a young age, so I did the next best thing. I cut them off myself."

I couldn't believe my ears. I didn't *want* to believe my ears. Jake had cut off his own breasts? It was almost too much for me to handle. How could he do such a thing and survive? There had to have been severe bleeding, and there is no way he could have had any medical training. And, I didn't even want to think about the pain he must have felt. How could he have done that?

I didn't have to wait long for my answer because after he walked me back into the bedroom, he excused himself and went into the kitchen. When he returned, I noticed that he was carrying a jar like the kind my mother used to keep jelly in.

Those must be the preserves Coco was talking about, I thought. But I couldn't have been more wrong. True, something was preserved in the jar, but it wasn't jelly...it was Jake's breasts.

"I've had these for many, many years now," he said, as he stared at the jar proudly. I probably would have gone to medical school if I hadn't been destined to do this. I've gotten better at it each time."

Now I was really afraid and confused. How many pairs of breasts did he have? There was no way he could have grown new ones, so what did he mean when he said he got better each time? I was still afraid to speak, but I decided that I might have to risk getting another beating if I was going to find out what I wanted to know.

"Jake," I whispered, "I don't mean to be rude, but how can you get better each time when you only have one pair of breasts?"

And then, I waited.

Instead of him slapping me though, he asked if I felt well enough to walk with him into the kitchen. I really didn't feel so good, but I had to go with him because I wanted to know what was in there. So, I slowly followed him to the kitchen.

When we got there, he told me that there were some more cabinets around the corner where he kept his valuables, and that was what he wanted me to see. I didn't really know what valuables had to do with what we had been talking about, but I told him I didn't mind looking at them anyway.

So, we walked around the corner.

I saw a large wooden cabinet that had writing on it. As I got closer, I could see that the words were from Song of Solomon in the Bible. It was the same scripture Coco and her friends had been arguing about the first time we met.

"'Your two breasts are like two fawns, twins of gazelle, which feed among the lilies,'" I read aloud.

"That's right, Jemimah," Jake said, as he went to the cabinet and started opening the doors. "A man would sell his soul to have a woman with perfect fawn like breasts," he continued, "which is why I made sure none of my girls ever looked like that. I wanted them to be more than just sexual objects. I wanted them to be able to make money off of more than just their chests. And they did…they did."

As he opened the cabinet, I saw rows of jars just like the one he used to keep his breasts in. At first, I didn't understand what I was seeing or why he decided to show them to me, but then it hit me. All of the jars in the cabinet were filled with the same things that were in his jar. They were filled with breasts, the breasts of the girls who worked for him. I wanted to turn around and run as fast as I could, but my body was too weak.

My head was spinning, and I wished someone would have pinched me and told me I was dreaming. No one did though. This was all real, and it was then that I realized why Jake had invited me to his home. I planned on keeping my breasts on my body and not in a jar, but if it was up to Jake, I wouldn't.

17.

I love my breasts.

I liked them before, but ever since my ordeal with Jake, I love them so much. I know I'm, young, but I think having breasts is what makes a woman sexy. It also makes us unique. I mean, men have breasts too, but they can't get milk from theirs. Hopefully, I'll have a baby one day, and when I do, I definitely want to feed it with my breasts, especially since I almost lost mine. Besides, who cares if a man likes to look at a woman's chest? Sometimes it's flattering, if he's not staring too hard.

I wish Jake could have understood that having, or not having breasts, didn't make him a man or not make him a woman. His problems were a lot deeper than that, but he never saw it. He never dealt with the things that happened to him during his childhood, and that's what drove him crazy. I've been going to counseling, and that's one of the things I learned. I have to deal with the past in order to have a future. Jake's past never left him because he never let it go. The sad thing is, he hurt so many people because of it.

I almost threw up when I realized what was in those jars he had. How could he take something that was so precious from so many people? Who gave him the right to play doctor on innocent people? I didn't know the answers to those questions, but I did know that I wasn't going to be his next patient. I was going to leave that house, whether I was in pain or not. I would rather have bruises all over my body than no breasts.

I bet that's how he got the other

girls' breasts. He probably beat them so badly that they couldn't move, and then he did his crazy operation. The whole thing was a setup. He knew what he planned to do to me from the first time we met. I couldn't believe how stupid I was. But now that I knew what was happening, there was no way I was gonna let him get me. No way.

"Jake," I said, after I pulled myself together, "what happened to all these girls?"

"The ones who survived the surgery worked for me. You'd be amazed, Jemimah at how many men actually thought my girls were erotic. Many men were turned on by their lack of breasts, which was sickening, but then what else would you expect from a man?"

"But how was this helping your sister? Weren't you doing the same thing to your girls that her pimp did to her?"

He slapped me. Hard.

"You are such an ignorant, ignorant child," he said through clenched teeth. "How could you think that what I was doing was even remotely related to the things my sister had done to her? Her pimp used her. She was nothing more to him than a piece of meat. When her looks started to fade because of the drugs, he killed her. *My* girls had self-esteem. *My* girls understood that the shape of their bodies had nothing to do with their sensuality or sexuality. Their power was in their minds, not their breasts. Yes, they had real power, just like a man."

I didn't say a word. My jaw as throbbing from the slap he had just given me, and I didn't want to get hit again. I had to think of a way to get out of his house though. We were in the kitchen, which meant we were closer to the front door than we would have been if we were in the bedroom, still, it wasn't close enough.

I decided I would try to talk to him to see if I could change his mind. I didn't have anything to lose, (except my breasts), so I gave it a shot.

"Jake, you really don't want to cut off my breasts because they don't look like the ones you have in there," I said, as I pointed to the jars in the cabinet. "They're not the size of fawns, or any other animal. Well, maybe a hamster, but that's not very big. My breasts wouldn't even be worth the trouble," I added.

I held my breath and waited for him to speak. He didn't say anything at first, and I could hear him taking long, deep breaths. I didn't see what he was doing because I had my eyes closed. If

Jake was going to hit me again, I didn't want to see it, so I just stood there with my eyes closed and waited.

"Have you been paying attention to anything I've said to you in the last two days?" he asked. I could tell by the sound of his voice that he was really angry. "It's not about the size of your *breasts*, you imbecile; it's about the size of your *brain*. The size of your worth and self-esteem. Sacrifices must be made in order to receive power. It's only when one has given up that which renders him powerless that he can obtain power."

"But my breasts haven't rendered me powerless, Jake. As a matter of fact, my breasts have gotten me work and kept me from going hungry. Isn't that a good thing? Doesn't that mean anything?" I was pleading with him at this point, but I didn't know what else to do. I knew if he tried to perform surgery on me that I would die. Things in my life hadn't always been so great, but I didn't want to die. I wanted to be able to make a change in my life. I wanted to know if I *could* make a change and if I could find happiness. And, I wanted all of my body parts when I did it.

"What if I promise never to turn another trick? Then can I keep my breasts?" I asked. "Isn't that what all this is about anyway? Aren't you just interested in prostitutes who make a living off their bodies? Well, if I'm not a prostitute anymore, then you don't have to worry about that happening to me. I was thinking about quitting anyway, and since Kilo left me money when he died, I can live just fine without turning tricks."

"Jemimah, I'm not going to

argue with you. This is not debatable. You were the one who followed me around, remember? You were the one who just couldn't leave me alone, even when Coco told you to. You wanted to be close to me. You wanted to work for me, and now you have your chance."

I couldn't argue with that. I did keep after him, even when he treated me like trash. I thought we had some kind of connection. I thought we understood each other, or at least I thought he would understand me. The only thing I understood now, though was that Jake probably trapped many girls the way he trapped me. He used his looks, just like the girls he cut up used theirs. But, he didn't see anything wrong with what he was doing. He truly believe the he was helping the girls out by destroying their bodies. If that was the way to get their power, then I didn't want it.

I wanted no part of it. All I wanted
to do was go back to the hotel, get
my things, and go home.

18.

The first time I testified in church, I told the congregation about what happened to me at Jake's house. Most of the saints were so shocked that they hardly knew what to say to me at the end of the service. I'm sure some of them didn't believe what I had said, but those who did talk to me said the story was too weird for me to have made it up. It was too bizarre to not be true.

I felt blessed to be able to talk about what happened because I almost didn't make it out alive. At least, I didn't think I was going to. I'm usually a kinda quiet person, but when I went to church that night, I was determined to say what was on my heart.

"I'm not very good at talking in front of a lot of people," I began, "but I decided before I left home this evening that I was going to give my testimony tonight." I could feel the tears welling up in my eyes, and at first I tried to hold them in, but when one of the saints said, "It's okay. We all been there sister," I let them fall.

"I never really understood what it meant to be blessed until recently. I used to hear people say it was a blessing to be alive, but for most of my life, I didn't feel that way. I spent so much time being used and abused by so many people, that I had begun to wonder why I was alive."

I had to stop right then because the memories of my dad and the things that happened overtook me, and I couldn't speak. After a few seconds though, I was able to continue.

"I've lived in some of the

worst places and done some of the worst things you can imagine."
Then I told them just a little about some of the things I had to do as a prostitute. I wasn't sure if I should have gone into as much detail as I did, but I felt like I needed to make them understand how far I had come.

"There was a time in my life when I thought a man could save me. I thought a man could give me the love I never had with my family, especially from my father. Looking for that kind of love almost cost me my life. I haven't talked about what happened with anyone, but since you are the only family I have, I want to share it with you."

And, I did.

After I tried pleading with Jake not to hurt me, I decided that the only thing left for me to do was try to run away. It was obvious that

he wasn't going to let me leave on
my own. He was determined to add
me to his collection of preserves,
and I was determined not to let him.

"It's really hot in here, Jake.
Can I go sit on the porch for a little
while?" I asked.

"No."

"But I've been in this house
for a couple of days, and I really just
want to get some fresh air. I won't
try anything Jake, I promise. You
can come with me."

"Sit down, Jemimah," he said.
"I have to think."

I went in the "dining room"
and sat down on one of the wooden
chairs. My body had started to ache
all over, and I really wanted to go
back to bed, but I couldn't. If I got
comfortable or laid back down, I
might not ever get up, so I sat there
and thought.

Jake had stayed in the kitchen, and I realized that it had been a while since I had heard anything from him. He was very quiet…too quiet, and that made me nervous.

"Jake," I said, "are you okay?"

Silence.

"Jake, did you hear me? I said are you okay?" I didn't want to, but I knew I was going to have to get up and go to the kitchen. I was afraid that as soon as I stood in the doorway, he would start chopping at me with a butcher knife, but I got up anyway and walked slowly to the kitchen. When I got to the doorway, I hesitated, and that's when I heard him.

At first, I thought he was asleep because his breathing was slow and deep. When I got closer to him though, I could see that he was crying. He was holding one of the jars of preserves in his hands and staring at it like he saw something in it that he hadn't seen before.

I didn't move.

"'For my thoughts are not your thoughts, nor are your ways my ways, says the Lord,'" Jake said. "'For as the heavens are higher than the earth, so are my ways higher than your ways, and my thoughts than your thoughts.'" By this time, he had turned around and was looking at me. I saw the tears rolling down his cheeks, and my heart went out to him. I almost felt like hugging him…almost. Instead, I stood in the doorway and waited for his next move.

"You're wrong about me, you know," he said, after a while. "I'm not a vicious person. Nothing I do is motivated by hatred. In fact, it's quite the opposite. Every one of the girls whose breasts I have, I loved.

You don't understand my ways.
You *can't* understand my ways
because my ways and the Lord's are
the same. But even Jesus had to give
up the ghost when his time was at
hand."

I didn't know what he meant
by that, but I knew that something
else was about to happen. If I had
been thinking clearly, I would have
taken that opportunity to run away.
Jake was sitting down, and I was
standing in the doorway. I could
have backed up and then run out the
front door, but in the condition I
was in, I didn't know if I would have
been able to outrun him if he had
decided to chase me.

"Do you know what Jeremiah
1:5 says?" he asked.

I didn't, but I knew he was
going to tell me.

"It says, 'Before I formed you

in the womb, I knew you; before you were born, I sanctified you; I ordained you a prophet to the nations.' That is your fingerprint of destiny, Miss Jemimah. It was mine, and now it's yours. I've spread my message to many, many people. I have been a prophet to the nations. Now, it's your turn. It's your turn to spread the word. It's your turn."

After he said that, he took a pad and paper from off the table and started writing. I couldn't see what he wrote because he used his hand to cover up the side of the paper that was facing me. When he was finished, he tore the paper off the pad and folded it up.

"One of your biggest problems, Jemimah, is that you don't listen. You may hear what a person is saying to you, but you don't listen. You assumed that I was going to cut off your breasts because of the things you saw here today and yesterday, and probably because I said you have to make sacrifices in order to gain power. But, did I ever say I was going to remove your breasts?"

He hadn't.

"Don't say anything because we both know the answer to that question. I've said more than enough in the last 2 days. You've learned all you need to know about how the world works, and what you need to have, or not have, I should say, in order to gain power. I just hope you don't bury your newfound knowledge under a bushel. Now, if you would be so kind, would you give me a few moments alone?" he asked, as he got up and walked to what seemed like a bedroom. "I need a little time to regain my composure because it has been hectic around here since your visit. I give you my word that I will allow you to leave as soon as I have had a chance to collect my thoughts. Is this satisfactory?"

I told him it was.

I went and sat down on the floor right next to the front door. Everything that had gone on between us over the months since we met had left me exhausted. I had never been in the Army, but I felt like I had been in a war. I didn't know what hurt more, my body or my brain. Jake was definitely a person who wasn't easy to forget, but I had decided that after that night, I didn't ever want to see him again.

I waited by the door longer than I intended. I guess I was so exhausted by everything that had happened that I fell asleep. When I woke up, I called out for Jake, but he didn't answer. I was really sick and tired of his stupid games, but since I knew I wasn't ever coming back there, I played along.

"Fine," I said, "I guess I'm being disobedient because I called you instead of coming to get you like you asked. Well, forgive me please." I know my tone was sarcastic, but I didn't care. I headed back to the room where he had gone, and the door was closed. I figured he probably dozed off the same way I did.

"Jake," I whispered, as I lightly tapped on the door, "get up." "We both fell asleep, but I'm ready to go now." While I was talking, I turned the doorknob and slowly opened the door. There were no lights on, so at first, I couldn't see anything. I started rubbing on the wall trying to find a light switch, and when I did, I saw everything.

Jake was dead.

He was hanging from the ceiling with a note pinned to his chest that said in big black letter, "IT IS FINISHED."

I screamed.

I screamed and screamed and screamed, and I didn't stop until I had passed out.

geveryl

GOD

19.

I didn't know if Jake had any next of kin, and even if he did, I didn't know them, so after regaining consciousness, the only place I knew to go was to the salon. I left Jake where I had found him because I didn't know what else to do. Besides, I didn't know how to explain to the police why I was there. As soon as I walked into the salon, Coco came over to me, and by the look in her eyes, I knew that somehow, she knew.

"Coco." It was all I could say before I collapsed on the floor and began crying uncontrollably. I felt like I could never be able to cry out all the tears inside. My eyes were hurting, and they were probably swollen too, but I kept on crying. I wrapped my arms gently around my knees and just slowly rocked my body back and forth.

"Jem," Coco said, "Baby, it's all right, but you're going to give yourself a heart attack if you keep crying like that. Besides, you're slobbering all over my floors, and I just mopped."

I started to cough then because I had started laughing while I was crying, and it was making me choke. After a while though, I was just laughing.

"Come on. Get up girlfriend and come sit over here with Mama Coco."

Slowly, I got up and went to her booth. My body was still very sore, but I didn't resist when she pulled me onto her lap and wrapped her arms around me.

Coco just held me close to her and rocked me gently. I could feel her lightly rubbing her fingers through my hair, and it almost made me cry.

I hadn't been held like that since I was a child. I remember how my mother used to sit me in her lap and rock me in an old rocking chair that she said belonged to my grandmother.

Finally, I pulled myself together enough to tell he what had happened.

"I knew the end was near for Jake," she said. "He just wasn't himself. He had started acting strange. I mean, strange even for him. I tried to talk to him, but it was no use. I can't see him dying any other way, though. It was his destiny."

Even though Coco joked around a lot, I could tell Jake's suicide really upset her. They were like family, even though they fought all the time. He really didn't have anyone else in his life, which is what I said when I told her I had left him hanging in the bedroom.

"Diva don't!" she yelled. "Don't *even* tell me that you just left the man swinging from the chandelier. Oh, that is ruthless. Why didn't you call the police, or at least an ambulance?"

"Because I was scared. I didn't know what to do, Coco."

"Well, I'll take care of it," she said.

And she did.

Coco took care of everything even the funeral arrangements. No one was sure if Jake wanted a funeral, or if he wanted to be cremated, but Coco thought everyone deserved a proper send off, so she paid for a funeral.

She told me that Jake had

gone to a church called Shepherd's
Fold, and as far as she could tell, he
liked it a lot. She said he liked the
pastor, and the people in the
congregation made him feel
comfortable. I hadn't been in a
church since I was little. Kilo's body
was cremated because that was the
only thing I knew to do for him. I
didn't keep his ashes though.

Anyway, the day of the
funeral, I was nervous. I don't know
why. I guess I wasn't looking
forward to seeing him after the way I
had seen him the last time. I had
trouble sleeping since his suicide,
and I hadn't eaten much either. I
kept seeing his body every time I
closed my eyes. I hated him for
doing that to me. I hated him for
picking me to spread his sick
message. Still, I felt like I kinda
owed it to him to go to his funeral.

When I got to the church, I

was surprised at what I saw. Most of
the people there looked like me. We
didn't look like twins or anything like
that; they just looked like street
people. A few of the girls I thought
I recognized from my
neighborhood. There were quite a
few people at the funeral, and a lot
of them looked sad. I guess it never
dawned on me that Jake might have
had friends.

I liked the church. It
understood what Jake meant when
he told Coco he felt comfortable
there. I hadn't even talked to many
people, but the ones I did speak to
were very friendly. They seemed
happy to see me, even though I had
never been there before.

I was so busy looking at all
the people and being greeted that, at
first, I didn't notice the beautiful
casket at the front of the church. It
was white, and it had little gold lines

running along the edges. On top of the casket was a huge flower arrangement filled with red and yellow roses. As a matter of fact, there were flowers everywhere. It was hard to see the pulpit because the flowers were covering everything.

One of the ushers came over to me and asked if I wanted a program, and when I looked at the program, I had to bite my tongue to keep from screaming out loud. It wasn't because I was shocked at seeing Jake's face, it was because the face on the program didn't look anything like him. As a matter of fact, it wasn't him at all…it was her.

20.

I couldn't believe my eyes. The picture on the program was of Jake as a woman. And…his name was really Mary. Mary! I opened the program and read about Jake/Mary's life. It said he had a twin sister named Martha who preceded her in death. It didn't really mention much about Jake's parents except that they were dead too. In fact, the program didn't say much about Jake's life at all. I wasn't surprised that it didn't mention what he did for a living, but oddly enough, it did say that she was "affectionately known as 'Jake' by her friends."

One of the ushers got up and recited a poem she had written, and I was glad that it was written on the back of the program as well because it was so beautiful, even though it didn't rhyme. It was called "Does Beauty Ever Fade?" and after she got finished reciting the poem, I couldn't stop thinking about the words.

Does beauty ever fade?

Not when its brightness

Is caused by the everlasting light of God's love.

Jake, our hearts are warmed

By the memory of your precious spirit

And the sweetness of your soul.

Tears of joy are flowing, for we know

That you are rejoicing with the Lord,

And your reward in Heaven is great.

Only a few can say that they were blessed

To have been in the presence of angels

For a short time in their lives.

We love you, Jake.

And the beauty of your love will shine in us

As our North Star to God.

After that, several people sang

solos, and a few of the members talked about what a kind and soft spoken person Jake was. Then, several of the women from the salon got up and told funny stories about the things they used to do with him. It really wasn't sad at all, until Coco got up to speak.

She looked beautiful, and I could tell that she was pleased at the way the service was going. She began by thanking everyone for coming and for all the nice things they had said about him. Then she told the congregation that she wanted to talk about a side of Jake that most people didn't get to see.

"I met Jake 5 years ago," she said, "and it was hate at first sight."

Everybody laughed.

"He came in looking all handsome in his suit and tie, and I wondered what in the world a good-looking man like him was doing in a nail salon. So you know I was floored when he looked me straight in the eye and said, 'I'd like to get my nails done, please, and I brought my own polish.' Now, I know some of you may think that was a weird thing, but for those of us who knew Jake, we understand."

I smiled.

"He was a complicated person, but he had a good heart. He would never intentionally harm anyone, not even an enemy. Everything he did, he honestly thought was done out of love, and maybe in his own way, it was. God knows, he could make me so angry sometimes that I wanted to knock his teeth out, but I never did. I couldn't hit him. At least not with my fist. I do recall a few times when I had to give him a severe tongue lashing, but that was only when he needed it."

I didn't want to cry. I didn't want to feel sad for someone who tried to kill me on more than one occasion, but I did.

I missed him.

"Before Jake passed away," Coco continued, "we talked about his relationship with God. If there was one thing Jake believed in, it was God, or Jesus I should say. He believed so much that it totally consumed his life. Now, I'm usually the type who likes to joke around and make wise cracks, but the last time we spoke, Jake said something to me that I will never forget. He was feeling depressed because he thought the Lord had forsaken him, or should I say, he thought he had done all that he could do, and that he was useless. He took his Bible out of his coat pocket and read from Isaiah 43:1. Not all of it, just the part that says, 'Fear not, for I have redeemed you; I have called you by your name; you are mine.'"

Coco stopped talking then because she was crying. "I'm sorry," she sobbed, "but this is really hard for me. I never thought I would have to do anything like this, and it just very difficult. Please bear with me."

Of course, everyone understood. Jake obviously meant more to Coco than even she realized, which made his death even sadder. I wanted to go up to the front to be with her. I didn't necessarily want to say anything; I just felt like maybe standing next to her, or putting my arm around her might make her feel better. I didn't go though. I just sat in my seat and cried.

I had been doing that a lot lately. Crying that is. But as time went on, I realized the tears I cried were helping me become a better person. That probably sounds a little corny, but it's true. Everything that happened to me made me stronger. I had to grow up, which at 16 wasn't easy.

While Coco was pulling herself together, I notice that the woman sitting next to me was staring at me. I tried not to look directly in her face, but she was making me uncomfortable. After a few minutes, I finally turned to her and said, "Why do you keep staring at me?"

"I'm sorry," she said. "It's just that you have such a beautiful spirit. You're a beautiful person, and I couldn't help staring. God loves you very much."

I was speechless.

No one had ever said

anything like that to be before. I didn't even know what she meant by "beautiful spirit." She kinda said it like she thought I was an angel or something. I didn't know what to say, so I just told her I liked her dress, and then waited for Coco to start talking again.

"As I was saying before," Coco continued, after she had regained her composure, "Jake truly believed that he had been called by God to do something special in the world. He believed everyone has a purpose, a destiny, and his was to make people feel good about who they were, no matter who they were. No, he didn't think like most people thought, and he didn't do things that most people would do, but he always had the best intentions, no matter what. Not many people got to see Jake as much as I did. He was a special person, and I just wish he knew how special he was himself.

The last time he came to see me, he was discouraged, and I really didn't know what to say to him. Since that time, however, I found a scripture in the Bible that says everything I wish I had said to him that day."

Then she opened her Bible, turned toward the casket and began reading.

"'For a mere moment I have forsaken you.

But with great mercies I will gather you.

With a little wrath I hid my face from you for a moment;

But with everlasting kindness I will have mercy on you.Says the Lord your Redeemer.'"

"I love you, Jake," Coco said. "I'll see you in Heaven."

After she got finished, the church was completely silent. I don't think anybody could talk because we were all too busy crying.

No Shoes and Platforms got up to speak next, and when I looked on the program, I saw that their names were really Tasha and Beverly. I was kinda glad they were up next. Sure, No Shoes and even Platforms could be really rude at times, but they were also very funny, so I was hoping that just like Coco had made everybody cry, No Shoes and Platforms would do just the opposite.

They did.

"Look, y'all are gonna have to stop doin' all that cryin' and snottin' all over the place. Jake wouldn't want none of that. He wouldn't want any of you to mess up your make-up, especially not the pretty ladies," No Shoes said.

"That's right," Platforms continued, "Jake was fierce from

head to toe, and I was one of the ones who made sure he stayed that way. Even though he was soooo handsome, I can't tell you how many times we both had to repent because he made us cuss."

"Honey when he was around," No Shoes said, "I was in a constant state of PMS, but I loved him anyway."

It was funny how quickly the mood had shifted in the church. One minute, we were almost about to have an emotional breakdown, and the next, we were laughing hysterically. It was the strangest funeral I had ever been at. Actually, it was the *only* funeral I had ever attended. I didn't even go to my mom's. Anyway, we laughed at all the funny things No Shoes and Platforms said and did, and by the time the pastor got up to do the eulogy, no one was sad anymore.

21.

When the pastor went to the pulpit, I was a little caught off guard. First of all, he was young. Not a teenager, but not 35 or 40 years old either. At least he didn't look like it. He was also very cute. He had dimples that you could see even when he wasn't talking, and he was at least 6 feet tall, with a muscular body. If I had seen him on the streets, I would have definitely approached him.

I couldn't believe that I was lusting at a funeral, but I was. Once he started to speak, however, I forgot all about my sex thoughts. He may have looked like a young man, but he spoke like someone who had been in the world a long time. His voice was so deep and so strong that he didn't even need to use the microphone. He came down from out of the pulpit and stood beside the casket. Then, he turned towards the casket and just stood there with his back to the congregation.

The church was silent.

"I knew Mary," he began, as he slowly turned around to face the congregation. "We went to elementary school together. I knew her sister Martha as well. I remember playing with them both on the school playground at recess. Martha always wanted to be the leader, or whoever was in charge. But Mary? Mary just followed along behind her sister like the rest of us."

He was smiling, but I could see that he was hurting too. Even though he was facing us, he never took his hands off the top of the casket. He was stroking the roses that were on top, but I don't think he knew he was doing it. It was like he was somewhere else. Somewhere far away.

"I knew Jake too, except I didn't know Mary and Jake were the same person... not at first anyway. I remember I ran into Jake at the supermarket, and when he stopped me and spoke to me, I just thought he was someone I had met through the church, or at a minister's conference or something. But then, I took a good look at his face, and it looked like the *face* of Mary, but she had the body of a man. Nevertheless, when I asked if she was Mary, she just smiled and said, 'I should have known you would have recognized me after all these years, David.' I hadn't seen her since we were children, so she didn't know I was a minister and that I pastored a church. Of course, I invited her to worship here, and she came. She came at least 2 Sundays a month for the next 5 years."

I really liked the pastor. Not because he was cute, although I have to admit that did have a little to do with it, but because he seemed like a genuinely nice person, and not someone who pretended to like you in our face and then talk about you as soon as you left. That's probably why Jake kept coming back.

"In the years that Mary attended church here, we had numerous conversations about the Lord. We didn't always agree; in fact, we never agreed, but we didn't argue either. She just thought about things differently than I did. Come to think of it, she thought about things differently than most. But I loved Mary, and I knew Mary, and that's why I can't stand here today and sugarcoat the way I feel right now. I know people want to hear a sermon about how the angels in Heaven are rejoicing and singing around the throne because another one of God's children has gone home, but I can't tell you that. I can't preach that because that is not what I am feeling, and it's not what the Lord wants you to hear."

Then he told us to get our Bibles and turn to Isaiah 59. He said if we didn't have a Bible, which I didn't, then we should look on with our neighbor.   My neighbor, of course, was the lady who had been staring at me because I had a "beautiful spirit," so she was more than happy to let me look on with her. The pastor had a big Bible that almost looked like it would be too heavy to hold, but he picked it up and was holding it open with one hand. *He must lift weights*, I thought. Then I wondered if he was married.

"Before I continue," he said, "I want to let those of you know who have never been here before, that I am led by the Spirit. The

Spirit of God, that is. I am just a messenger, for the things I say aren't from me, but they are from God. These are not my words, just my voice speaking the utterances of God."

I believed him. He seemed like the kind of person God might speak through because he seemed to be really holy. So, I just read along in the Bible with my new friend, and for the next 45 minutes, I listened to one of the most unusual sermons I've ever heard in my life.

22.

I went to get my nails done today. It had been almost 2 years since Jake's death, and I felt like I was ready to go back to the place where we first met. Besides, I hadn't seen Coco since the funeral, and I wanted to tell her how well things had been going for me lately.

When I got there, I was surprised by how different things looked. Actually, the salon wasn't different, just bigger. Coco had opened up her boutique in the back, and there were rows and rows of platform shoes, bell bottom pants, vintage clothes, and the most beaded jewelry I had ever seen in my life.

"Well, well, well, the prodigal daughter returns," Coco said from behind me.

I quickly turned around,

grabbed her, and gave her the biggest hug that I could. She lost her balance a little because of the way I grabbed her, but she didn't fall

"Let me guess," she said, after she had caught her breath, "you're happy to see me, right?"

"Coco, you know I am. And I bet you're happy to see me too."

"Yeah, yeah, yeah, I'm ecstatic honey. Can't you see the excitement written all over my face?" she said sarcastically. Then she started to smile, and I knew she was glad I was there.

"So, come on diva, sit down and give me the juice. Dish, dish, dish. I want to hear it all."

So, I told her everything. She knew I had started going to Shepherd's Fold after Jake died, but she didn't know I had joined the choir. She didn't even know I could sing. No one did, really. I'd always had a nice voice, but as a prostitute, I didn't get many opportunities to sing.

"You really are a diva," she said. "Come on, let me hear you sing something, Miss Ross. Make me reach out and touch somebody's hand. Let me know that ain't no mountain high enough, girl."

"You're still silly, Coco," I laughed, and I was glad she was. Even before Jake died, I could always count on Coco to make me laugh, especially when I was feeling down. It's not like she was my personal clown or anything; she was just a naturally funny person. But sometimes I wondered who she talked to when she was sad. Coco was always so good at cheering other people up, so I wondered who cheered her up.

I never asked her about that

though. Whoever it was obviously did a good job because she was upbeat most of the time. Today was no exception. I wanted to ask about Jake, but I didn't know how to bring it up. I could tell she wanted to talk about him because she went out of her way not to mention his name. Finally, I asked her if she ever thought about him.

"All the time, Jem. All the time. I know I joke around a lot, but you know I really loved Jake. I really did…still do. I just wonder if he knew how much I cared," I could tell by the look in her eyes that she wanted to cry, but she didn't. Instead, she looked at me and said, "Now see what you did, Jem? I was fine until you came in here and made me all sad. And girlfriend, I was even about to cry, and you know I must never smear the Maybelline."

I   laughed,   and   then   I

apologized for almost making her "unDivadize" (that's a word she made up) herself. Then I told her that it was all right to say Jake's name. It was okay to talk about him. In fact, that was why I had come.

"You know, Coco," I said, "I still think about Jake almost every day, and even sometimes when I'm out working."

"Working? Honey, I thought you were all sanctified and everything. You ain't got no business working nothing but your brain, so you can get a real job. I better not ever catch you out on the street 'cause you know Miss Coco will pimp slap the taste out of your mouth, and you know I will."

I did know she would. I told her I do have a real job working in the church office. I just do filing and other small things, and it keeps me busy. However, I have turned a few tricks when money gets tight, and I told her I don't do that very often at all and that I'm still being delivered from prostitution.

"It's a process, Coco," I explained. And even though it had been almost 2 years since I got off the streets full time, I still had 4 years of being on the streets and all the years of abuse at home still inside me. I guess it all went back to me not being able to forgive myself and not remembering that when it came to God, nothing I had done before mattered. But, I was much better than I was a year ago, or even a month ago, and each day I was getting stronger.

"I'm still gaining knowledge and understanding. I'm still on a spiritual journey," I told her.

"Well, you just better not be trickin' along the way, that's all," she said.

Then Coco asked me if I was just going to sit there and talk without getting my nails done. I told her I wanted to do both. We talked about lots of different things, but I really wanted to talk about the sermon Min. Aiken preached at Jake's funeral I couldn't get the things he said out of my mind after all this time, and I wondered if she could either.

"I remember almost every word," she told me.

So did I.

23.

Behold, the Lord's hand is not shortened

That it cannot save;

Nor His ear heavy,

That it cannot hear.

But your iniquities have separated you

from your God;

And your sins have hidden His face from

You,

So that He will not hear.

For your hands are defiled with blood,

And your fingers with iniquity;

Your lips have spoken lies,

Your tongue has muttered perversity.

     Isaiah 59:1-3. That was my favorite scripture now. Most people usually picked something like the 23rd Psalm, but it has been my favorite scripture ever since I heard

it at Jake's funeral. That's what Min.
Aiken had us turn to in the Bible
that day, and that's what he spoke
about.

"When I first read that
scripture at the funeral, I didn't
know what it meant," I told Coco, as
she was about to start my manicure.
Actually, I kinda did know what it
meant, I just didn't know why he
would choose something like that to
talk about at a funeral. I was
expecting him to choose something
more upbeat and positive, instead of
a scripture that sounded so bad.
But, then like he said, those weren't
his words. Min. Aiken was just
reading what God had told him to
read, I guess.

One of the ladies in the
church actually stood up and read
the scripture out loud, and after she
got finished reading, the church was
silent. No one made a sound. They

were probably all wondering the same thing I was. Min. Aiken closed his Bible slowly and laid it on the altar next to Jake's casket. Then he started walking back and forth while rubbing the bottom of his chin, like he was thinking real hard.

"You know, when he started walking around in front of the church," Coco said, "I started wondering if he was crazy. I had never seen anyone just stop and walk around like that."

I told her that I had thought he was just really thinking about what he was going to say next, but she still insisted that he might have temporarily gone a little nuts due to grief. Then I stopped talking because I began to think about what Min. Aiken said after he stopped pacing.

My heart is heavy today Saints of God. My heart is heavy because my sister is dead. No, Mary wasn't my biological sister, but she was my sister in the Lord…was. There was a time when Mary understood about the mercies and grace of God. There was a time when she realized that there was no problem too great, or no situation too difficult for God to solve. But, somehow along the way brothers and sisters, somehow, Mary got lost.

It was weird hearing him call Jake, "Mary." I never could get used to the fact that Jake was a woman. Even when he showed me his breasts in that jar, it still seemed too bizarre to be true. But, he was a woman: a woman who had many, many problems.

"How long did you know about Jake?" I asked Coco, while she was massaging my hand.

"I knew as soon as I saw him. Mama knows, chile," she said. "Mama knows."

My massage felt good, and my mind drifted back to Jake's funeral and the sermon.

I read Isaiah 59 to Sister Mary the last time we spoke. She had come to me because she hadn't been able to hear the voice of God like she once had. She was upset because all of her so called 'good works' were being 'taken out of context,' as she put it. I know God loves everyone, but there is something her that no one seems to want to realize. Mary was a child of God, that much is true, but she was also crying out for help, and Saints, we failed to hear her.

"Why didn't you tell me about the 'preserves,' Coco?" I asked. "I almost threw up when I saw them."

"You wouldn't have believed me if I had," she replied, "which is why I didn't. You would have been ready to have me institutionalized if I had told you that Jake had a collection of 'titties in a bottle' on display."

She was right. Still, I wish I had been prepared. But then again, I don't think anything could have prepared me for that. So, as Coco continued doing my nails, I thought about the next words Min. Aiken said at the funeral.

Some of you may not have known about the life Sister Mary led, but most of you did. Most of you were here the night she came and poured her heart out to us. We knew about her pain; we knew about her suffering, and we knew about the pain and suffering she had caused others. Yet, we kept silent.

"Did you ever go to church with Jake, Coco? Were you there that night, when he gave his testimony?" I asked after a few minutes.

"I went with him a couple of times, and I liked it," she said.

"And, I was there that night. He had asked me to go with him for moral support, you know. But chile, I didn't know he was gonna spill his guts. Honey, he told those saints everything. EV-E-RY-THING."

That's when it dawned on me that most of the people in the church already knew about Jake, and that's why they didn't seem surprised about my testimony. The ones who were shocked were probably the ones who weren't there the night Jake had come. Things were beginning to make a lot more sense to me now, and as I went back to thinking about Min. Aiken's sermon, I couldn't help but wonder how Jake's life might have been different, if someone in the church, or just anyone had not kept silent.

The Bible says that the Lord thinks thoughts of peace and not of evil towards us. But, we must seek Him and search for Him with all our heart. We cannot lean unto our own understanding because we will never be on the same level of understanding as God. Never.

24.

It made me sad when I thought about how much Jake believed he was just like Jesus. It made me even sadder to think the he believed Jesus got pleasure out of tricking people. He must have been in so much pain for so many years to actually believe that.

"What happened to Jake's parents?" I asked.

"Your guess is as good as mine," Coco said. He never liked to talk about them, and I didn't blame him or push the issue. His dad was disgusting, and he never said much about his mother, well, just that she was dead. Of course, I knew about what had happened to his sister, but that's about all I knew. I wrote Jake's obituary, and I knew more than anyone else seemed to know about him. Well, maybe Min. Aiken knew some other things about him, but that's about it."

Well, one thing was for sure, Min. Aiken definitely didn't have a problem talking about the things he did know about Jake, and he was so blunt about it that it was a little shocking.

Mary was a murderer. Oh, she may not have physically killed people; although, she said that she had, but she was a murderer of souls, which is a more terrible crime. But, we loved her. We loved her because we knew and understood that she was doing what she thought was the will of God. She was being obedient. Even in her wrongdoing, she was willing to heed the voice of the Lord.

We both agreed that we were shocked when Min. Aiken called Jake a murderer. That wasn't a very nice thing to say about someone who was alive, and it was even worse to say it about someone who was dead.

"Miss Jem," Coco said, "I almost choked when he said that. Girl, I had to fan myself real hard to keep from fainting. I know I won't be able to hear what people have to say about me after I'm dead, but I know I don't want *him* to say one word. Oh, he got better as the sermon went on, but that one statement was enough to put him on my 'people who should keep their mouths shut at my funeral' list forever."

I laughed, but she was right. Everybody knew Jake had faults. We all have them, but I didn't see why he had to say that about Jake, especially at his funeral. But, there was a point Min. Aiken was trying to make, and eventually, he did.

What I'm trying to say is that Sister Mary had the kind of heart that we, as Children of God, should have. Even though we know that causing harm to others is wrong, and that God doesn't want us to do think like that, how many of us would be willing to obey anyway? Do you understand what I am saying? How many of us would obey God, without question, when we know it's Him speaking to us, and we know He's telling us to do the right thing, even it if it's something we may not necessarily want to do?"

I hadn't thought about that before. Jake always insisted that everything he did, he did out of love. He always believed that he was destined by God to live the life he had made for himself, and he did. Jake made no excuses. He understood what he was supposed to do, and he did it. Most people, like me, don't even know what they are supposed to do with their lives.

"What's your destiny, Coco?" I asked.

"Weeellllll," she said slowly, "it

seems like I'm destined to have people work my nerves. They started bothering me early this morning, and they haven't stopped yet. Let's hope tomorrow my destiny changes."

"Come on, Coco," I pleaded. "Don't you ever wonder why you were born? Don't you ever think about things like that?"

"Yeah, sometimes I do, and I know Jake believed in destiny, but I believe that whatever a person is doing at the moment is his or her destiny at the time. I don't think there is just one thing that a person is supposed to do in life, and then that's it. That's not cute. That's not cute at all because after you've done your one thing, then your life would basically be over."

That was a good point; however, I still believe that everyone has a special duty to perform that only that person can do. Maybe I would change my mind as I got older, but for right now, that is what I believe.

I started thinking about the end of Min. Aiken's sermon as I went over to the wall to pick out my nail polish. I always said I thought Jake would be a part of my destiny, and he was.

So, Saints of God, we must do what the Lord would have us to do. The spirit must lead us. The Holy Spirit will never lead us astray. So when our lives are over, we can rest assured knowing that we have finished our course, and we have fought the good fight. Sister Mary fought a battle, but the war was within her. Somehow, along the way, she lost sight of the fact that Jesus was with her. He never left her, even when she felt alone. Sister Mary forgot that Jesus was wounded for our transgressions and bruised for our iniquities. The chastisement for our peace was upon Him and by His stripes, we are healed. We are healed from every affliction, Saints. Be it physical or mental, we are healed. So, I stand before you today, grieved in my spirit. I have grief because I know that my sister died without peace. She died without joy, and she died without ever realizing that her life was in God's hands.

Min. Aiken gave an altar call after that, and that's when I decided to give my heart to God. I didn't want to die the way Jake had. I didn't want to let the pain of my past determine my future. So, when Min. Aiken asked anyone who wanted to know the Lord, and who wanted to know real love and real peace to come down to the altar…

I went.

Coco and I sat and talked for at least 3 hours that day. It normally didn't take that long to do my nails, but we had a lot of catching up to do. When I went over to the wall to pick out a polish for my nails, I didn't see Really Raspberry as a choice of colors. I was a little surprised at first, and I started to ask Coco why it was gone, but I didn't. Instead, I just looked over at her, and when our eyes met, I immediately understood why it was gone. No one else needed to wear that color again, and hopefully, no one else ever would.

ABOUT THE AUTHOR

Geveryl Robinson, MFA, is a native of
Baltimore, MD and a former English professor
and Op/Ed columnist for the Savannah
Morning News. She lives and writes in
Atlanta, GA.